A Rebel's Daughter

The 1837 Rebellion Diary of
Arabella Stevenson

BY JANET LUNN

Scholastic Canada Ltd.

Arabella Stevenson
Monday, 11 December, 1837
Stevenson House
Toronto, Upper Canada

Dear Diary,

I have brought this wretched diary out from the drawer in my desk, a thing I never, ever thought I would do, but I shall not write to a book as though it were a human person. Definitely NOT. But I must write or I shall burst. (Ha! Mama cannot see what I have written. There, I will write it again, B-U-R-S-T.) Oh, but what has happened is worse than writing every last vulgar word in the entire English language — worse than absolutely every last thing you could imagine in the entire world. Papa is in the gaol, Charlie has disappeared, and we are in disgrace and I have no friends and nothing is right at all. And that horrid Mr. Mackenzie has run away.

There! I wrote that name Mama said was never, ever, to be mentioned in our house. Mackenzie. WILLIAM LYON MACKENZIE. I hate him. What happened is all his fault for writing those horrid things about the legislature in his *Constitution* newspaper and making good men like Papa agree with them. But I truly do not believe Papa agreed with them. I truly do not. It is a terrible mistake that Papa is in the gaol. Papa was NOT a rebel. He was a reformer. I heard him say that. The government men will soon find this out and Papa will be home.

Sophie says there is talk that none of the rebels will go free. She says "them as don't get hanged, Miss Belle, are certain sure to be sent off to that prison island way down to the other side of the world." She does not know where it is or what it is called but there are gigantic birds there that feed on people. (The Saylors' footman told her that.) Convicts are sent there. People who have stolen things and murdered people. Not barristers like Papa. This will NOT happen to Papa. Papa is NOT a rebel. He will soon be set free. I know he will be.

There has been a stupid rebellion against the government. Part of it was almost right here in Toronto. Just last week! A great mass of working men and backwoods farmers with rifles and pikes and clubs came marching towards us from north of the city. They almost got right into the city. We were all terrified. There were battles (but not right in the city). Some men were killed and houses were burned. The rebellion is over now (well, it is over in Toronto). The government men won and Papa is in the gaol — but that is a mistake.

Dr. Strachan denounced the rebels from the pulpit in St. James yesterday but we were not there to hear him. I expect I should be glad we were not. I found out about it today in school. Mama refuses to leave the house. She has taken to her bed with a cart-load of smelling salts.

Now I have smudged the precious diary. I am NOT going to cry! I swore on Papa's big Bible that I would not cry another tear and I will not!

Later

I have had my supper. It was stewed mutton (from the roast at dinner, I expect) with potatoes and carrots, and apple tart for afterwards, but Mama did not come down, Charlie is not here and Papa — oh, everything is so horrible!

Even later (past midnight)

There is no fire in the grate and it is very cold but I cannot sleep. Today in school was — it was — it was just horrible! Everyone was absolutely, completely, totally hateful. I wish I had stayed at home.

"Oh, Arabella, it is too dreadful. Your own father. How you must suffer." Spiteful Maud Adams said that.

I was walking up the front steps behind her, hurrying because it was so cold, and she turned right around to say it. Then she sniffed and turned her head away and went into the school. Mary Spencer actually pulled her skirts away from me, but Mary always does absolutely everything Maud does. Neither of them spoke to me again all day.

Nor did anyone else. Not a single girl was willing to stand my friend. It is not that I was the most popular girl in school (I do not believe one can be popular if one is not precisely pretty AND is good at sums) but I did have friends. I thought I had friends, but not even Jane or Patty spoke to me yesterday. Patty slipped a note into my hand at closing time. She wrote, *"My mother will not permit me to speak to you. I am devastated."* She signed it, *Love, Patty* and put a whole row of *X*'s and *O*'s but that did not make me feel one bit better. I walked home alone and it was snowing. I did NOT cry.

Interruption. Dolly just jumped into my lap. She does not like it when I write — or when I read. She plumps down on my lap and shoves herself between me and the book. She sits there like a tall grey shadow. Now she has stalked off twitching her tail because I pushed her away — I had to, I need to write this.

I do not suppose it matters about the girls not speaking to me (except for Jane and Patty), as I am not going back to that school. This afternoon Miss St. Clair sent a horrid note around to Mama. It said:

Toronto, Upper Canada,
1837

I think it would be best if Arabella were to withdraw from the Miss St. Clair School for Young Ladies.

I can hear her say it in her high, stuck-up English voice. Miss St. Clair thinks no one born in Upper Canada can be as fine as people born in England — which, of course, is just as Mama thinks. So I do not find it difficult to conjecture what Miss St. Clair must think of a girl whose Papa is in the common gaol.

I will never return to that school, not even when Papa comes out of the gaol and everyone wishes to be my friend again. I could never have imagined this happening to me. How can I bear it? For once in my life I think as Mama thinks, "What is to become of us?"

Well, what is?

Tuesday, 12 December

Dear Diary,

There, I have done what I said I would not do. I have written to you as though you were a person. I must talk to someone even if it is a bundle of blank pages. I wonder if I should give you a name. Perhaps Rosamond after the girl in the story about the purple jar? I like the name Rosamond even if I do not much like that story.

Dear Rosamond — no, not Rosamond.

Perhaps Naomi after the good woman in the Bible?

Dear Naomi — no, not Naomi.

Perhaps Mr. Great-Heart from *The Pilgrim's Progress*, but I think of you as a girl, a girl to confide in.

Well, I suppose I must say Diary and consider that a proper name. I wonder if, the next time Dolly has kittens, I might call one of them Diary?

I did not wish to think of you this way because, when Aunt Parley in England sent this book to me last year at Christmas, a picture of Augusta Milroy hopped into my head. I could see her little yellow ringlets bobbing up and down, up and down, while she jabbered on about her DI-I-I-ARY with its "ADO-O-O-RABLE tiny golden latch." Now here I am writing in a DI-I-I-ARY and it HAS a little gold latch. Just like Augusta's (but I do NOT think it is adorable).

Well, Diary, if we are to be friends, since I know what you look like, I had better tell you what I look like. Then you will know my outsides as well as my insides (well, to be precise, my inside thoughts). To be honest, I do not truly wish to tell you what I look like because Mama says that my looks are the despair of her life. Charlie is handsome — which, I presume, is why Mama prefers him (of course, he is a boy). He is tall, even for fifteen, and has fair, curling hair like her own, but he has brown eyes like Papa's. And his face is long like Papa's — and mine.

I have dark hair like Papa's, which I sometimes

wear in a plait down my back. My eyes are grey and neither large nor small. My mouth is too wide (Mama says) and my face is pale. I am not well favoured, Diary, but, I am pleased to relate, neither am I especially ill favoured, and my voice is pleasing enough. I am short of stature for my age. (Did I tell you that I am twelve years old? I am. I became twelve last August the thirteenth.) I am only a trifle over four feet and two inches and I fear that I am VERY thin.

I am not thin because I am given to physical exercise. I have no desire to run or skip rope or climb trees with the boys as my friend Patty does (my erstwhile friend Patty). Nor do I wish to play battledore and shuttlecock or swim with Charlie as Patty and her sister Caroline do with their brothers. I am perfectly content to applaud them in their games when they require someone to do so. This is not because I think, as Mama does, that these activities are not suitable for young ladies, it is because I am of a more contemplative nature. No, that is not true. Diary, I shall be honest with you, I am completely not interested in sporting activity. I do like to walk, and to skate in winter but, otherwise, I prefer to read books or play chess with Papa than — oh dear, I do not suppose there are any chess boards in the gaol.

Dear Diary,

I fear I left you with a dangling thought last night but I am sure you understand why I did so. I am full of resolution this morning.

First I mean to describe to you where I am — perhaps I had better say where we are. We are in my bedroom and the sun is shining through the big window that looks out over the front garden and Lot Street (I consider Lot Street the pleasantest street in Toronto). There is a cosy fire in the fireplace and I am sitting at the desk Granddad made for me two years ago from the maple tree that crashed to the ground in a lightning storm on his farm. It still bears, just a very little, the scent of fresh wood. I love my desk.

I love our house, too, but it seems so big now. There is not a soul here but Mama and me. (Sophie and Mary and Peggy are here, of course, but they are all below stairs.) Mama keeps to her rooms all the time, even for meals, and no one comes to visit. No one. It is so lonely. I suppose I ought not to be too surprised that Jane does not come because she is even more timid than I, but Patty is not. If she were in my place, I would find a way to see her, no matter what Mama said. I know I would. How can she be so cruel?

Everything is like a horrible dream — but what if it is all true? What if Papa does not ever come out of

the gaol? What if Charlie never comes home? I know he was not with the rebels because the night the rebellion began he said he was joining Colonel Fitzgibbon but he has not been home since. What has happened to him? Wherever can he be? Diary, I am so frightened!

I wish we had gone to church on Sunday to remind God that we are in dire need of Him. (No, I do not, I have just remembered about Dr. S.) I pray every night by my bed but I am not sure God really hears us if we do not go to church. I could almost wish to ask Sophie if I might go with her next Sunday, even though she goes to the Roman Catholic Church and I would have to sit with the servants, but I am not sure if even Sophie would want to be seen with me.

I pray for us all, but especially for Papa. I miss him fearfully. Papa is quite serious. He does not laugh a lot, but when he smiles, it is the most wonderful thing. When Papa smiles, it is better than a whole week of birthdays. I love him so much. We have such good conversations together — he talks to me as though I were grown up. We talk about books — Papa loves poetry, which I own I do not always understand, except for the funny sort. We talk about gardens and geography and mathematics and, last year, when Gran and Granddad died in the week after Christmas from the diphtheria, we talked about them and about dying and I felt a little less sad afterwards.

We have oftentimes talked about the law because I find it very interesting. I like things to be fair, which is what I think the law is about. Papa cares about fairness, too, which I suppose is why he chose to become a barrister. In fact, sometimes Papa shouts and beats on his desk with his fist when he talks about things that are unfair. But Diary, then why would he be one of the rebels? Being a rebel, going about shooting people, is not a single bit fair! (You see, I cannot entirely keep from my mind the thought that Papa MIGHT have been one of them.)

Later

I left you, Diary, because my ink bottle was almost empty. I went downstairs to fill it from the master bottle in Papa's study and to sharpen my pen. It was so cold in the study with no fire, that there was a film of ice on the ink. I could smell baking so I went down to the kitchen. It was warm and cosy there and Sophie had made scones. We had scones and tea together. I love to talk to Sophie, even though Mama does not like it. (Mama is so particular about not being friendly with servants! I believe sometimes she really thinks she is a duchess. Once, when Papa was shouting about Mama's extravagances, he said she spent money as though he were as rich as a duke. I think Mama acts as though she had married a duke

— and not just because she spends so much money.) When I was very little, Sophie told me I could call her Sophie even though everyone else said Cook. We have been friends ever since that day.

Sophie told me that other wives and families are taking food and clothing and blankets and such to the men in the gaol. I went straightaway to Mama to ask if we might take these things to Papa and she had a fit of hysterics. (I should have known she would.) She will not send a servant or even listen to talk of it. I shall admit to you that it makes me shudder to think of going near the gaol. It must be a horrible place. Papa is a gentleman so he must have been given extra blankets to sleep under and better food than the common men. I hope the blankets are thick ones because Papa is really quite thin. But, Diary, Papa does not have his books, not even his Bible. Someone must take him his Bible.

Friday afternoon, 15 December (at my desk)

Dear Diary,

I did not write on your beautiful pages all yesterday or last night because I was in a "slough of despond."

This is what happened. After I wrote that someone needed to take Papa his Bible, I could not tear the thought from my mind — or that the someone would have to be me. I knew Mama would not do it and I could not ask the servants, not even Sophie, as she cannot walk that far because of her rheumatics. (I really believe that she does not walk because she is so stout.)

So I resolved to go. I waited in my room yesterday morning until I felt sure that Mama was not going to demand something of me. Then it was almost noon so I waited until after dinner. I read the story about Mr. Fearing in *The Pilgrim's Progress,* to make me feel brave. I was so apprehensive, I could scarcely even look at my dinner. (You may as well know, Diary, that I am not brave.) I had to eat. Sophie would know that there was something amiss, were I to leave even the smallest morsel, because I always eat everything — even creamed potatoes, which I do not like. So I ate an entire dish of rabbit stew and then gingerbread and I drank my tea. But I did not want it.

Right after dinner, I put on my best cloak, the marine-blue one with the fur lining, but not my best bonnet as I did not wish to draw attention to myself (it has a beautiful peacock's feather wrapped around the brim). I went into Papa's study. I took the Bible from his desk and shoved it under my cloak — it made such a huge bulge that I was glad no one was in the hall to question me. Out I went.

Outside, it was cold, cold, cold! and the wind was so strong it almost blew my bonnet off. People were walking very fast and I only saw one man on horseback all the way to Newgate Street. The little Saylor boys were chasing each other in front of their house but they did not seem at all merry to me and, for the first time ever, the bells on the sleighs did not seem to sing such a bright song. I kept my head down so that I would not see anyone turning away from me. I clutched my cloak (and Papa's Bible) tight to myself and trotted along almost as fast as the horses. I was scared but I kept going because I did so want to give Papa his Bible.

I did not see Papa. The gaol is a fearsome place. I had to walk by the area where the gallows stand whenever there is a hanging. It was horrible. I felt a bit sick. There were guards outside, with muskets on their shoulders, marching back and forth. I stood there until one of the guards (a really tall one with a bristly moustache) looked as though he meant to approach me. I fled. And now Papa does not have his Bible. Diary, I am so ashamed of myself.

Saturday afternoon, 16 December

Dear Diary,

How I long for this terrible time to be over and everything to be as it ought to be! Mama lies on her chaise longue all day having Mary bring her tea and then, of course, her vinaigrette, because she just knows she will faint. Then she sends for me so that we can "beweep our outcast state" together. Yesterday, after the beweeping, she told me to send a note to her friend Mrs. Whistler to come to her "in her time of trial." I said I would and I did begin to write the note but, Diary, I could not. Julia is in my class in school. I could not make myself write to her mother. I do not believe Mrs. Whistler would have come, in any case. Else would she not have done so already?

Still Saturday, but now it is night

I am so worried about Charlie. My brother is such a torment to me when he is at home, but now I long for him to be here. Do you think he has gone haring off on some wild chase? Papa says Charlie is a hot-head and one never knows what he will do. But he might be hurt or — no, I cannot think about that. Oh, Diary, I wish I knew what to do about anything!

How can we bear this great burden? Whenever someone dies or is ill or is even stuffed up with a common cold, Great-Aunt Laura Henry says that. And then she clasps her hands together and looks at the ceiling.

Good night, Diary, I am going to bed.

Well, I did not go to bed. No, that is not true, I did go to bed but I did not stay there long. I sneaked downstairs and retrieved five (FIVE!) candles from the drawer in the pantry. (Is sneaked a proper word? Miss Latchmore is not here to instruct me, so I do not suppose it matters. Still, I like things to be correct. And orderly. And proper. I like things to be done the way they ought to be done. I could never, ever be a rebel. Not ever!)

I took this many candles so that I can write all night if I wish to. I should say, if I MUST, because I cannot sleep and I NEED to write and write and write. Writing to you makes me feel better. Also, Diary, perhaps if I tell you about the horrid rebellion, I might understand what has brought us to "this sorry pass" (something else Great-Aunt Laura Henry says). This is something else about me, I need to understand things. Mama says that I am too inquisitive for my own good but, truly, I do need to know things.

I wish I knew how to start a fire but, Diary, the only time I tried to do so, all I achieved was so much smoke that I alarmed the entire household. So I am bundled into my dressing gown, my shawl (the pretty rose-coloured one) and the quilt from my bed — and I am sitting on my feet.

I shall tell you everything I know, which is not everything there is to know because, you see, no one at school talked about William Lyon Mackenzie or rebels or reformers. Mama thinks "political matters" are not fit for female ears and Papa never spoke of them to me. So I only know what Sophie or Mr. Jenkins told me or what I overheard Papa and his friends say about what happened before the fighting began

Oh, I am sorry. I did not mean that *n* to run all over the page. Dolly jumped into my lap and startled me. Of course, I had to stop to cuddle her (her fur is so soft!).

This is what happened twelve days ago, just after midnight on Tuesday, the fifth of this month. We were startled awake by ringing bells. We were up from our beds and in the front hall before the hand in the hall clock could reach the next minute — Mama and I and the servants. Charlie came racing in through the back entrance shouting, "It's rebellion! Mackenzie and at least a thousand men are out at Gallows Hill and they're on their way to the city."

He said that Colonel Fitzgibbon was gathering the loyal militia to fight them. Mama grabbed his sleeve to make him tell us more but he pulled loose. He shouted at her, "I've no time to talk! I'm off with Fitzgibbon," and he dashed out through the big front door. Peggy and Mary flew out after him. So did Dolly.

Mama was shrieking and calling for Papa. I went chasing after Dolly. Outside, the bells were very loud. People were running every which way. Some had hats. Some had coats. Most were in their night-clothes, their shawls half covering them and their hair flying. They were shouting and crying, "War! War! We shall all be killed! We are doomed!" and other things I do not remember. The shouts were loud. The bells were louder. It was fearfully cold and my feet were bare so I ran back inside. I did not find Dolly until the next morning.

The next morning Sophie told me that Mackenzie and a "messa rebels, Miss Belle" (Sophie talks like that) "were a-comin' down Yonge Street as if old Nick himself was after 'em."

She said some of the rebels captured Mr. Alderman Powell and another man in Yonge Street out at Gallows Hill. (I think G. Hill is about three miles out of the city.) What happened was as exciting as a story in *The Gazette*. Alderman P. had pistols hidden in his greatcoat. He waited for his chance, then he sneaked a pistol out of his coat and shot one of the rebels dead. In a flash, he yanked his horse around and galloped at top speed down towards the city. Suddenly there was William Lyon Mackenzie riding STRAIGHT AT HIM. Alderman P. pulled out his other pistol and fired right into WLM's face. But the pistol did not go off. Imagine that!

Alderman P. charged off. When he got to the New Road, he jumped off his horse and hid behind a big log in the woods until the rebels were gone. Then he ran (I expect his horse had bolted) back onto Yonge Street and all the way down into the city to warn Sir Francis.

Diary, if you could see Alderman P., you would never in your life imagine that he might have an adventure like that. He is old and VERY stout. I think those rebels were not very clever. They should have made him get off his horse and they should have searched for his pistols.

Also it was very cold but the road is not frozen hard yet. I wonder that all those running men and galloping horses did not fall and slide all over themselves because they must have made the road very muddy.

The newspaper Papa reads said that the rebels shot a man that same night way out at the Eglinton Crossroads, outside a tavern. That tavern belonged to Mr. John Montgomery and it is famous now because there was a battle there a few days later. The tavern is gone now because the government men burned it to the ground.

We did not know about it all on that night, but the bells ringing and Charlie shouting about rebellion gave us all the shivers and shakes. We were sure those rebels would march straight through the town to Front Street and burn every house along the way and murder us all.

Now I am sleepy. I will write more of this story tomorrow.

Good night, Diary.

Sunday morning, 17 December

Dear Diary,

Here I am again. I fell asleep last night with Dolly purring in my ear and I slept all night long. I do not know what I dreamed but I think it was pleasant because, when I woke up, I felt like smiling. I think my dream did not know about the rebellion.

The story, continued:

In the morning after the night with the bells and all the racing around, government guards were everywhere, and every house, shop and big building in the city was closed and most were boarded up. I know this because I went out to see.

Mama paced up and down the hall almost all morning. She was dressed but her hair was loose and hanging down her back. She kept wringing her hands and moaning and shrieking, "Oh, that wretched man, where can he be? Where can he be? How could he be away from home at such a time?" Finally she went upstairs to her room and I went out.

It was so cold I could see my own breath and the wooden planks beside the street creaked under my feet, but it was bright and not windy. The windows on houses and shops were boarded up but there were people everywhere. Some of them were dressed so this way and that and looked so dazed I thought they must not have gone to bed at all. I did not stop to ask anything. (Does this not surprise you, Diary?)

I was so eager for word of Charlie that I went straight down to the college. Henry Buller (one of C.'s classmates) was on guard out front. You could see, by the way he was parading back and forth, that he thought himself the most important person in the world — and Henry Buller is almost as short as I. He told me that Alderman P. and a party of men had ransacked WLM's print shop in Palace Street and that there was a guard on his house in York Street. Henry said there were more than 5,000 armed rebels marching towards the city and not more than 300 loyal men to fight them. (Almost all the soldiers from the garrison left last month to help stop the rebellion in Lower Canada.) He said that Sir Francis and all the government officials were in the marketplace preparing for battle and a lot of the boys from the college were there, too.

Off I went to Market Square. I could not get near the men because of the guards and three farmers with pigs and a cow that had got loose, but I found Will Saunders, who is another of C.'s classmates. He thought C. was with some others out in Yorkville Village at the tollgate. I was not prepared to walk all the way out there so I went up to Duke Street to see Mr.

Jenkins. (He is our shoemaker. Charlie threatens to tell Mama that I visit Mr. J., whenever C. thinks I mean to tell when he sneaks out with his chums to watch a cockfight — as if I would!)

Mr. J.'s shop was boarded up and there were four guards outside the bank and post office. I asked a woman who was talking to one of the guards what was happening, and all she could tell me was that Sir Francis's whole family was keeping safe aboard a steamship out in the bay. Diary, I shall confess to you that I longed to be in that ship with the governor's family. I was, as Sophie says, "some frighted."

I scudded home as though I had wheels on my feet and all the way home I was hoping, hoping, hoping that Papa would be there — but, of course, he was not.

I suppose I should have known where he was. I can see, now that I am writing this down, that I have been deceiving myself, telling myself that Papa was not a rebel. I might have known better because of all I heard last summer.

My hand is cramped from writing and it is almost dinnertime. I hope Sophie has baked a chicken.

Sunday night

Dear Diary,

You are my salvation. Writing to you keeps me from been absolutely terrified.

I think Papa might have started to be a rebel when Cousin Matthews first came to the house. (Cousin M. is a distant relative but Papa calls him cousin. His Christian name is Peter.) Mama was very cross about him coming to visit. I heard her tell Papa that Cousin M. was naught but a common farmer and that she did not care to entertain him. Papa said that he would never turn his cousin from his door. I think Papa felt angry. I felt angry, too. Granddad was a farmer and I loved him — and he was NOT common. (If they were still alive, I wonder what Gran and Granddad would think about Papa being in the gaol.)

Of course I had to look at Cousin M., after what Mama said. (Mama says that I am an atrocious eaves-dropper and I own it is true but, if I were not, how would I learn anything?) So, that day, I sneaked into the hidey place beside the drawing room where we used to play hide-and-go-seek. It is perfect for watching people in the drawing room because there is a thin sliver of space at the back where the two walls do not quite join.

Cousin M. was sitting in the armchair by the long front windows and Papa was sitting across from him on the loveseat. When I squinted my eyes, I could see them, and I could hear them quite clearly (but I do not remember a single word they said). I thought Cousin M. VERY large and not at all good-looking. He only wanted to talk about politics, which you know is a very dull subject of conversation. Perhaps that is why Mama says it is not a suitable subject for females.

I must correct myself. Politics is not dull. Politics brought this woeful misfortune upon us. And misfortune is NOT dull!

Interruption: I am so hungry I am going to look for something to eat.

Here I am again. Pray excuse the breadcrumbs, Diary, and the spot on your clean page. It is some of Sophie's best-in-the-world rhubarb preserve. Now I shall get on with the account of the rebellion. (Is it not amazing how bread and preserve makes one feel better about absolutely everything?)

Cousin M. came again a few weeks later and brought another man with him. (Mama was exceeding cross.) I did not intend to listen to them because, to tell the truth, I still thought politics dull. I was looking for Dolly — she goes into the hidey place when the door is left open. She was not there and I was set to come out when I heard Charlie in the hall. He had his odious friend Jesse Harvard with him. They stayed for the longest time trying to make up their minds about what to do. I was stuck so I could not help but hear Papa and the other men in the drawing room.

They were sitting close together by the fireplace. Of course there was no fire in it but, still, I could not understand why they did not sit by the open windows because the day was so warm — and the scent of roses and geraniums from the front garden is wonderful.

They were talking about the House of Assembly and Mr. Robert Baldwin. (Once we went to a New Year's reception at Mr. Baldwin's Spadina House.) They said Mr. B. was a reformer. They talked about something they called the Family Compact and Cousin M. said that none of the Family Compact cared about the farmers and their crops or about anything to do with ordinary people in Upper Canada. He said that life was getting harder and harder for everybody. He pounded his hand so hard on the arm of the chair, I feared it might come loose.

Papa and the other man said they agreed. Papa said that his people had always been good, hard-working people. He was "whole-heartedly with the reformers, barristers like Mr. Baldwin and Dr. Rolph."

Diary, I shall confess that I grew really bored. I did not understand what Family Compact meant or much else they were talking about. Also, it was hot and stuffy in the hidey place. I fell asleep and did not waken until there was no one in the drawing room and it was nearly suppertime. I was really peevish!

Now I have fallen asleep and made that ugly blot on your beautiful page. I am sorry. I have ink on my fingers and on my nightdress and likely in my hair, but I cannot tell that because my hair is almost as dark as the ink.

Good night, Diary, I am going to bed. I hope I do not get ink on my pillow.

Monday morning, 18 December

Dear Diary,

Continued from last night:

Granddad's old neighbour from the country, Mr. Bowerman, came to call soon after Cousin M.'s visit. I had to sit in the drawing room with him because he asked to see "the children." (Lucky Charlie, he was not at home.) Mr. B. sat on the loveseat and he is so fat that a lot of him hung over the edge of it. After he finished telling me how grown up I was, he started the politics talk. He pounded on the floor with his walking stick and he said that the government would not help when the bad weather made the corn and peas and beans fail. He said he did not think those Family Compact men cared for anybody or anything but "their own worthless hides."

That was exactly what Cousin Matthews said, so then I had to know what Family Compact meant. I went to see Mr. Jenkins the next day. He told me that the F. C. is a group of men who are like a rich family that keeps all its riches for itself and does not share with anyone. He said that "they are very British in the way they think." I think they must be like Mama and

Miss St. Clair and Augusta Milroy's mother who think you are only important if you come from England (but not like Mr. J., who comes from England but has a different kind of accent).

So I suppose the reformers want to reform those F. C. men. Of course Papa would be a reformer because the F. C. men are unfair and you know how Papa hates unfairness. I shall not ever be able to vote because of being female, but, if I could vote, I would be a reformer and vote for Mr. Baldwin because I do not like unfairness, either. But I would NOT be a rebel!

Cousin M. came a few more times in the summer. Once he brought two other men. I think W. L. Mackenzie came the second time. I did not see him because I was upstairs, but Mama had one of her fits in the front hall. We could hear her all through the house. I could see her, too, because I went to watch over the stair railing. She was pacing up and down, shaking her fist at the drawing-room doors and hissing at Mary to fetch Papa.

When Papa came out into the hall, Mama grabbed him by his coat lapels and screamed, "If you do not get that dreadful man out of my house, I shall leave at once and I shall never return."

Papa sighed. He said, "Yes, my dear, I shall see to it," as he always does when Mama has one of her fits. Then he went back into the drawing room. The men left right after that.

I cannot remember if there were any more of those visits because King William in England died in June and "beautiful, young" Queen Victoria became the queen. To tell the truth, I do not think she is so very beautiful but Papa's newspaper said "beautiful, young." She IS young, though, only six years older than I, and I do think that is young for a queen. Imagine being only a girl and sitting on a throne and telling people everywhere in the world what to do!

All through August the city was covered in black *crèpe* to mourn the king — men all had black arm bands around their sleeves and women had black shawls or bonnets. I did not like all that black.

Then I had my birthday on August thirteenth. Papa gave me a copy of Mr. Bulwar's book, *The Last Days of Pompeii* (it is very interesting but sad). I had a new white gauze gown with pink rosebuds embroidered on it and a tea party in the garden. It was not too hot and the flies were not too numerous but we had to cover the dishes because of wasps. We had scones and cheese, tea cakes with strawberry preserve and a beautiful fancy cake and ices from Mr. Rossi's confectionary shop. All those girls who do not speak a word to me now were happy to come to my party. I wish that cake had made every one of them sick!

I forgot WLM and Cousin M. and Mr. Baldwin and the reformers and the Family Compact men all the rest of the summer. WLM and his "faithful followers" did not forget — but they gave up reform. They were making the rebellion instead. They were making it all summer and all fall. WLM had meetings all over Upper Canada. In Toronto they were in his print shop in Palace Street and in Mr. Elliott's tavern at Yonge and Lot Street and in Mr. Doel's brewery in Newgate Street. Nobody else knew about those Toronto meetings. But everybody knows now because the whole story has been revealed. Diary, do you think Papa was at those meetings? I KNOW he agreed with Mr. Baldwin and the reformers because I heard him say so in our own drawing room. Cousin Matthews said he was with the Reformers too.

I think Cousin M. must have decided to go with WLM and the rebellion men and then, I think, he persuaded Papa to go with them.

Diary, why would Papa — no, I am not going to think about that.

Good night.

Tuesday afternoon, 19 December

Dear Diary,

I left you in the middle of the story again and I am sorry. Here I am, once more. I have had another long, lonely, woeful day. I went down to the kitchen this morning to see Sophie but she was too busy to talk to me. She was pickling some pigs' knuckles that her sister's husband had brought from Belleville. I told her that I do not like pickled pigs' knuckles. She said, "You'll be glad enough to have 'em, Miss Belle," and she sent me out of the kitchen. So I came up here to sit at Granddad's desk and write on your pages. (And I will NOT be "glad enough" to eat pigs' knuckles! I do not even like the way they smell!)

Tuesday evening

Dear Diary,

Here is the rest of the rebellion story.

Two weeks ago, the night the bells and guns woke us all up, the rebels were out at the Eglinton Crossroads in Mr. Montgomery's tavern, all set to march down into the city. (That was the night Mr. Alderman Powell almost killed WLM and I wish he had done!) They did not march until the next day — the day I went out to look for Charlie.

WLM and some other rebels came down as far as Gallows Hill that day to meet a party of loyal government men who were waving a flag of truce. Imagine, a flag of truce, just as knights in armour did back in the time of castles! WLM was at the front of the rebels, sitting on a little white pony. (He is a very small man.)

The government men asked what the rebels wanted. (Just as those ancient knights did.) WLM said they wanted "Independence." I think he must have said more than that because, Diary, I am only twelve years old, but I know Sir Francis and all those Family Compact men were not going to have half of Upper Canada be a separate country. Also, the Queen would never permit it even if she is only eighteen years old.

So the government men turned around and rode back down to the city with their flag of truce. Later that day, the rebels (Papa's newspaper said they were "insurgents") marched down the road to Postmaster Howard's house and forced his wife to cook dinner for fifty men. Then away they went and burned down Dr. Horne's big house on Blue Hill near the tollgate.

(Diary, I did not actually know all this on that day, I learned it all from Sophie and from the newspaper.)

All night we could smell the smoke from that fire, and the flames rose so high in the sky we could see them from our back windows. Sophie told me that hundreds of people went out to watch, some of them on foot. I think the fire was very sad and I would NOT like to watch it burn.

The next day hundreds and hundreds of loyal men from all over Upper Canada came into the city to help the militia men fight the rebels — and hundreds and hundreds of rebels went to Mr. Montgomery's tavern to fight with WLM.

All day long we could hear fifes playing and drums banging and guns firing and smell the gunpowder from where the militia men were drilling over in College Avenue. We were all terrified. I wanted Papa and I could not stop thinking about Sir Francis's family safe in the steamship out on the lake.

The day after that, on the seventh of December, there was a fierce battle out by Mr. Montgomery's tavern. The government men marched out to the fight from Front Street in columns like a parade. They started in front of Dr. Strachan's palace (it is not really a palace but it is so big and fine, everyone calls it that) with two brass bands. I think the bands were playing "Yankee Doodle." Colonel Fitzgibbon and another army officer were on their horses behind the bands. Sir Francis was on a huge black horse and Dr. S. and his assistant were on smaller horses, between the officers. Dr. S. had on his long black robe. The columns of men with their guns were behind them. They did not look anything like soldiers.

They marched over to Yonge Street (not Dr. S. and his assistant) and straight up through the city and — and this is something I do not understand, Diary. People followed them, in carriages or carts or on foot, all the way out to the crossroads to watch the battle. People in their houses in Yonge Street leaned out of their windows and waved flags and cheered and whistled. I can understand that, but how could anyone wish to watch men kill each other?

I could not find Charlie so I went home. I went

down to Front Street to see the men at Dr. S.'s palace because I hoped I would find Papa or Charlie. You know that I did not.

That battle did not last very long but there WERE men killed or wounded. The rebels lost. Sir F. ordered his men to burn the tavern down and to collect prisoners.

There was another battle by the covered bridge at the Don River on the Kingston Road. (Cousin M. was at the head of the rebels in that fight.) The rebels lost that battle, too. That was the end of the rebellion in Toronto. Hundreds of rebels escaped into the woods in every direction and almost one thousand were marched to the gaol in King Street, and a good many other places where they could be guarded. One of the prisoners was my Papa.

Wednesday morning, 20 December

I could not write any more last night, Diary. I shall finish about that terrible week after I find Mama's lace cap for her. Here I am. I found the cap (which Mary had not stolen, as Mama was loudly declaring, it was lying on her chest of drawers, hiding under a silk stocking she had flung there in a rage). Also I have had my breakfast. There was porridge with no milk or butter but Sophie's toasted bread was good and she makes such heavenly rhubarb preserve.

I closed my door so that Dolly cannot interrupt me but she is howling outside the door so I may have to let her in.

Back to the rebellion story.

The morning after those battles, Mr. Dewhurst (he is Papa's law partner) came to tell us about Papa. I do not think he cared to be the person to do so. He did not once look Mama in the eye. He would not sit but stood only just inside the drawing-room door. He even stuttered a bit. He said, "M-M-Mrs. Stevenson, I-I am afraid I have b-brought you some distressing news." Then he told us that Papa was unhurt but had been taken prisoner after the battle on Mr. Montgomery's farm.

Now we do not know what will happen to Papa.

No more do we know what has happened to Charlie. When he did not come home the day after the rebellion began nor the next day nor the next, I became truly worried. Mama would not talk about it. Sophie told me to send Peggy around to the hospital, where the wounded men are, to ask for Charlie. I did that. He was not in the hospital. I am certain that someone — Henry Buller or Jesse Harvard or SOMEONE — would let us know if he had been hurt or — Diary, I am going to have to write the word — killed. No one has come, so, if he is unharmed, why does Charlie not come home?

WLM has escaped and so have some of his friends.

I do not know of anything unfairer than those men running away like thieves in the night while Papa and the others must be held in the gaol to await trial. Sophie says that there is word that some of the men will be hanged. I know that cannot be true. Sir F. could not be that cruel. I cannot believe that. I CANNOT.

There have been no more battles here in Toronto. I know that a lot of the rebels who escaped after the battles have been found and brought into the gaol. I know that there is more to do with the rebellion in other places in Upper Canada and in Lower Canada, but I have not paid any mind to anything that is happening anywhere else.

Diary, I need to tell you something. It is something I cannot tell another soul. I miss Papa dreadfully but I am really angry at him. I wish you could know how many times he has said to me, "Arabella, do not be so easily swayed by the harum-scarum schemes of your friends. Always trust your own judgement!" And now that is just what I think he has not done. And it is NOT fair!

Thursday evening, 21 December, the first of winter

Dear Diary,

Today, calamity struck! (This is not entirely true. Calamity struck when Papa went to gaol. Today it got worse — although I would not have thought that to be one bit possible.)

Mr. Dewhurst came this morning. When Mama would not rise from her bed, Mr. D. asked for Charlie. When I told him that Charlie was not at home, Mr. D. said that he would call later in the day. I was obliged to confess that we did not know where Charlie was. Then Mr. D. gave me a note for Mama from Papa and bade me good day.

I ran up the stairs with the note. Mama was lying on her chaise longue. She snatched the note from me. She tore it open and read it. She shrieked. She jumped to her feet and tore it into pieces. Mary got Mama's vinaigrette and did what was needed for her. I gathered up the pieces and ran into my own room with them to put them together on my desk.

This is what the note said.

My dear wife, I cannot tell you how deeply I regret the circumstances into which my recent actions have thrust you and our children. You may consider my actions hasty, ill-judged and inconsiderate. If so, you are most likely correct. All I can say is that I wish, with all my heart, that I had not placed you, Charles and Arabella in such a parlous position.

Everett Dewhurst has agreed to act on my behalf in all legal matters and has offered his assistance to you in every way possible until I am, once again, able to resume my work and position in society.

Your affectionate husband,
Charles E. Stevenson

That was everything the note said, Diary, just that Papa was sorry. He did not say that he loved us or when he might come out from the gaol — or anything. Diary, I did cry (just the littlest bit) over those torn-up bits of note. I put them in my desk drawer.

Mr. Dewhurst came again in the afternoon. "Well, Arabella," he said mournfully (it is my opinion, Diary, that Mr. D. would make a perfect gravedigger), "since your mother is indisposed, your brother is absent from home and you have no relatives living in the vicinity, I am afraid I must discuss this unfortunate business with you."

We sat by the fire Peggy lit for us. I shall not clear my throat a dozen times or clutch my neckerchief as Mr. D. did. I shall tell you (without what C. calls roundaboutation) what Mr. D. said. "I am afraid, Arabella, that your father's involvement with Mr. Mackenzie's rebellion has left your family destitute."

He said a lot about poor investments and great extravagances. (I do know what that means because Papa, who almost never loses his temper, has done so many times about Mama's great extravagances.) Then he asked if I understood what he was telling me. I said I did. He meant we have no money. No money at all.

Diary, I once fell on the ice when I was skating and had all my breath struck from my body. When Mr. D. said those words it was as if all my mind was struck from my head.

Mr. D. reached across the space between our chairs and took my hand. "Dear child," he said, "I am so very sorry to have to be the bearer of this unhappy news." He said that it might have been worse because some of the rebels' houses have been seized and their families thrown out into the street. He said that with the help of Mr. Baldwin, he had managed to save our house and that he would do everything he could to help us sell it for a good price so that we would have an income. He said he would advise us about settling somewhere and he said that he would do what he could to locate Charlie.

I do not remember what we said after that. I know that Mr. D. left because I was alone in the drawing room when the big clock in the hall struck six and Sophie came to tell me it was time for supper.

Friday, 22 December

Dear Diary,

Yesterday and today have been unbearable. I am so afraid. I need someone to tell us what is to be done. Since Gran and Granddad died, there is no one left in Papa's family but Great-Aunt Laura Henry and she is of no use at all. All Mama's relatives are in England. There is no one but Mama to say what we are to do, and she will not.

This morning Mama's Mary came to ask me who

was to pay her wages. I did not know what to tell her. I went to Mama and she told me not to trouble her about such things. She said that Charlie would have to take care of everything. I told her — and told her, and told her — that Charlie was not at home. After a time I had to leave her because I could not make her listen to me about anything.

I went to her again this afternoon but, Diary, she would not listen. She completely, absolutely, entirely would not listen. There was naught I could do or say. She said dreadful things about Papa. She kept asking for Charlie. She cried, she sobbed, she screamed, and all the while she kept saying, "What is to become of us! What is to become of us!"

I did not know what to do. I was scared. I think Robinson Crusoe must have felt the same way before Friday appeared. The servants all knew by this time that there was no money. Mary did not ask again, she just said, "I trust you will see to it, Miss Arabella, that I get the wages owed me before I leave."

You likely realize, Diary, that Mama was not going to be the one to talk to Sophie or Peggy.

Somebody had to. Me. I went down to the kitchen before supper to tell them that I did not know about the wages owed them but that I would find out. I thought this is what Papa would say because he is a good man — but, oh, Diary, maybe those Family Compact men were unfair, but I wish Papa had thought about how unfair this is to us. Who will mop and dust the house when Peggy goes? And Sophie — oh, I cannot bear the thought of Sophie leaving us.

"Don't you worry none about me, Miss Belle," Sophie said. "Right now you got enough with worrying about yourself and your ma." Then she told me to go to Mr. Dewhurst, he would know what to do.

Peggy cried and Sophie cried and Sophie hugged me. Diary, I do wish you could know Sophie. She is big and warm the way the kitchen stove is big and warm except that she is not black, she is pink. She even has pink hair — almost pink hair — and a lot of it is always tumbling out of the knot she pins at the back of her head. And she is jolly — well, perhaps she is not so jolly just now, but she is still kind and comfortable. I love Sophie. From my youngest days, I have gone down to the kitchen just to sit by the stove to watch her cook, and listen to her tell stories about the backwoods where she grew up. She has never minded me being there.

Sunday, 24 December

Dear Diary,

I did what Sophie said to do. Yesterday after dinner, I put on my best wool dress (the dark blue one with the red embroidery trim near the hem, the one I wear to church — the one I wore when I WENT to church) and my warm blue cloak and my black velvet bonnet with the peacock feather. It seems odd but I felt braver for it.

I walked to Papa's office in Yonge Street to see Mr. Dewhurst. It was cold but there was not much wind and my boots have thick soles. I was glad to be out of the house.

It was worse being in Papa's office than being in school the day after he was in the gaol. It was like being with Papa and not being with Papa at the same time. The office smelled as it always has done, furniture polishy and papery and tobaccoey (from the cigars Papa always smokes there). The high windows and the two big desks and the big leather-covered chairs were just the same but, somehow, it all seemed different. I felt as though I had no right to be there anymore.

Mr. Dewhurst was as polite to me as though I had been Mama. "Please sit down, Miss Stevenson," he said and he pointed to the chair by his desk. Then he asked Mr. James, the clerk, to "bring the young lady some tea." But I could not drink the tea when it came. When I told Mr. D. I was acting for the family (I heard Papa say that once), he sighed and said he supposed I was, at that. He asked if we had any word of Charlie. I told him that Peggy had gone to look for him at the hospital and that I did not know where else to look. Mr. D. said that he was glad C. had not been hurt — he had had no word, either — but that he would continue his efforts.

Then he promised to "make some enquiries regarding the sale of our house." He said, by his reckoning, our house and furnishings would bring us enough money to pay our debts including what was owed the servants, and keep us in what he called modest rooms until Mama could decide what she wanted to do. He said he would need Mama's written permission, "to initiate the proceedings."

Diary, I felt great relief that someone was going to look after all these things but I did not feel exactly wonderful — but I did NOT cry.

I spent all this morning with Mama trying to make her understand that we must do what Mr. D. says or starve in the street. It took most of the morning just to make her really understand that Mary has gone. (Mary left yesterday morning. She did not talk to Mama. She told me that she would return for her wages.)

Mama called Mary an ungrateful wretch and then she said, "Arabella, you will have to find me another maid." Every time I said anything about Mr. D. selling the house she had another fit of hysterics and sent me to the kitchen for more tea and her vinaigrette. She would not talk about signing the permission paper. She said, "Charlie will see to that."

Diary, it is NOT fair for someone my age to have

to do all this! I cannot go back to see Mr. D. today because it is Sunday. And it is Christmas Eve.

Saturday, 30 December

Dear Diary,

Another week without seeing anyone but Mama and Sophie — and Mr. D. Peggy has left now. Mama pulls and pulls on her bell. Sophie gets tired of that so she goes up to Mama. Then Mama demands this and that until, finally, this afternoon, Sophie told her, "Mrs. Stevenson, I am the cook. I am not your personal maid." Mama put on that voice that I think must be more queenly than Queen Victoria's and said, "Cook, you are dismissed from your post."

"No fear," said Sophie, "I am only here to look after Miss Belle. When you've settled yourselves in your rooms, I'll be off to my sister Millie in Belleville."

After supper

I went again to see Mr. D. the day after Boxing Day. I did not bother with my Sunday clothes. As I told you, it is not a long walk but I felt that everyone was looking at me (the rebel's daughter) at every step I took. I am not in charity with Mama.

Mr. D. said that he could sign for the selling of the

house but that he would prefer to have Papa do it. I was afraid he was going to ask me to go with him to the gaol but he did not. I cannot go near that gaol. I simply cannot do it, but I wish I had thought to ask Mr. D. to take Papa his Bible.

Sometimes I close my eyes and pretend that all the dreadful things have not happened. I imagine that Charlie will soon be home from the college and Papa from his office, that Mama is in her room dressing for dinner and that I can sneak down into the kitchen to discover what Sophie is cooking. But I can never make the dream last.

I am really sleepy, Diary, but I wish to tell you the end of the house-signing story before I go to bed. Mr. D. did go to see Papa and Papa signed the paper.

1838

Monday, 1 January, 1838

Dear Diary,

It is New Year's Day. We were not invited anywhere and we have had no callers. We did not go to church yesterday. We did not go to church last Sunday or on Christmas Day. In fact, we have had no Christmas at all. No carollers came to sing at our door on Christmas Eve, no one came to call on Christmas Day. We did not have cedar boughs on the mantels or stair railings so there was not even the scent of Christmas in the house. Mama did not leave her room all day. Everything was dark and dismal. Even Dolly kept out of sight. I could not keep from remembering the amazing Christmas we had last year with everyone at home and all those unexpected relatives arriving.

I had Christmas dinner in the dining room by myself. Sophie put a bit of cedar on the table to make it pleasing. She baked a hen. She beat the potatoes, and the creamed onion was very good. There was plum pudding. But I could scarcely swallow a mouthful, not even of the pudding. I am the forlornest girl in all of Upper Canada.

Friday afternoon, 19 January
In King Street

Dear Diary, dear, dear Diary, my only friend in all the world,

I am sitting on the bed in my little room (my very little room) in King Street. Please forgive the smudgy pencil writing — of course I could not bring my ink bottle with me — well, I expect I could have brought it, but the ink would soon be gone.

Our house, our beautiful house in Lot Street, is sold along with almost everything in it. Mr. Dewhurst found Mama and me these rooms on the top storey of a rooming house east of the well at Princes Street. It is past Mr. Marian's Bakery, Dr. Widmer's surgery and a few very untidy houses, NOT in the fashionablest part of King Street. Mama says the rooms are not fit for pigs. They are better than that, but they are not beautiful.

At first, Mr. D. said that everything we owned had to be sold. Then he relented. Sophie and her brother Bill (he came to take S. to Belleville) helped the carter move Mama's bed, her chaise longue and her dressing table and chair, the kitchen table, two kitchen chairs, the pine settee and a small bed from the servants' quarters for me (I think it was Peggy's bed). Also we kept the kettle from the kitchen, a kitchen teapot, a few of the servants' dishes, enough linen for the two beds, and the big blue Sèvres vase that Mama would NOT part with (she brought it from England when she married Papa). She tried to bring a plate and a cup and saucer from the Coalport china but Mr. D. said we could not break up the dinner set. She was very cross!

I think all of Papa's books were sold except for his Bible and dictionary. Diary, I have decided that Mr. D. is a truly good man. He is going to take Papa his Bible and he just seemed to know how much I wanted the dictionary and he gave it to me. He said I might keep some of my own books, too. I kept my small Bible and my prayer book, *Aesop's Fables, Lamb's Tales from Shakespeare, The Last Days of Pompeii* and *Pilgrim's Progress.* (I feared it might be a sacrilege not to keep that.) I did not mind leaving *Gulliver's Travels* — it is not the sort of fanciful tale I like. I took *Guy of Warwick* and *King Arthur* from Charlie's bookshelf. Then I put them back because I feared I was keeping too many. Then, when I was halfway down the stairs, I went back. Charlie will want them when he returns. Oh, Diary, where can he be?

I kept the rag doll Gran made for me when I was small and the little wooden owl that Granddad carved for Charlie and, of course, I kept you. We kept most of our everyday clothes. Mr. D. bought my party gowns and kid slippers for his niece who lives in the west near Lake Huron. Mama would not give up her ball gowns or evening slippers and she kept most of her jewellery. (She did not tell Mr. D. about the jewellery.) Everything else was sold and Mr. D. was right, there was enough money to pay the servants what was owing them and, if we are careful, there will be enough to pay for food and for the rent here for some time to come.

The house sale was yesterday. Oh, Diary, I HATED, HATED, HATED it! Mr. D. said I need not be there but I thought perhaps it was the proper thing to do. It was the saddest, forlornest, dreadfullest day you could ever imagine. Even the weather was sad. The sky was dark. The icicles all along the eaves were dripping like giant tears. It was as though our house were weeping. The snow was grey and there were huge black puddles in it. It started to rain just as I reached the front walk. But, as everything for sale was inside, the rain kept nobody away.

All our possessions were out on tables, upstairs and downstairs, all through the house. I meant to stay but I picked up my skirts and ran when I saw Augusta Milroy and her mother. I expect Augusta thought it was the entertainingest thing in the world to see all my things out on the tables. She likely bought some of them. If only she does not have my desk! What I wish is that she would prick her finger on one of my needlework needles and fall dead as that witch wanted the sleeping princess to do in the story!

Interruption: I needed to go into the other room to get the knife to sharpen my pencil. I miss the pen and the ink although there is naught to spill with a pencil. I am glad I thought to bring that knife.

Mrs. Dewhurst, who is the busiest person in the entire world, took Mama and me home the night before the sale. Mama hated being at Mrs. D.'s house — she considers the D.s to be vastly inferior to us Stevensons because they do not have as much money as we have (as we did have, to be correct). They live in Graves Street and, worst of all, they have eight children, which Mama says is "positively indecent." In fact she hated being in their house so much I think she was almost glad to move to these rooms. (I daresay

Mrs. D. was every bit as glad.) Truly, these rooms are not fine (and they are none too clean and they smell of old cabbage and fish and other things I cannot discern but which are not pleasant). There are three rooms. Mama's bedroom is the largest and it has her bed and her chest, her chaise longue and her dressing table. It has a small window that looks out onto a bedraggled garden. Over the rooftops beyond it, one can see the lighthouse, the windmill and, closer, what is left of the old parliament buildings in Berkeley Street. At first, some of the rebels were being kept prisoner there. Mama had me close the shutters at once.

The other two rooms are smaller. This one (the front one) has the bed for me and a small chest of drawers. (I cannot keep from thinking of my pretty room at home with the pink wallpaper with the daisies all over it and my lovely four-poster bed with the white canopy — and my desk.) The middle room has the table and chairs and the settee, a dresser for dishes, and a small stove for heating and cooking. Of course, Mama will not cook. I do not doubt that I shall have to learn to do that if we are to eat anything but raw food.

Dolly has gone to live with Sophie in Belleville. Mama would not hear of bringing her. Oh, Diary, it was so hard saying goodbye to Dolly and Sophie. Sophie and I hugged and hugged and I fear that I cried a little — I think Sophie cried, too. She said she wished she could take me to Belleville with her. I wished it, too. When we left to spend the night with the D. family and Sophie went back into our house I thought the absolutely last worst thing in the world had happened. As events have turned out, it was not the last worst thing. I shall tell you about that "anon."

We came here today, after dinner at the D.s' house. Mrs. D. and Anne and Jenny came to see that we were "properly settled in." (A. and J. are nicer than ALL the girls at school. A. is a year older than I and very quiet, J. is a year younger and not quiet. She bounces. She is full of questions and ideas and talks all the time.)

I think this was exceptionally good of Mrs. D. because, truly, Diary, she is like a mama hen with too many chicks, always trying to keep them under her wing while they run about every which way. She even clucks like a hen — a cheery hen.

We made the rooms as pleasant as we could. Mrs. D. had brought a bit of tea, a loaf of bread, some butter and some preserves for our supper. Jenny put some greenery left from their Christmas in a dish on the kitchen table. But Mama did not notice. She went straight to her room. She did not say thank you or goodbye to Mrs. D. and she ordered me to come to her at once. I said goodbye and thank you to Mrs. D. and A. and J. then I went to Mama. She was lying on her bed with her hand at her head. She said,

"Arabella, I must have a maid. You will have to find me someone." Then she sighed and closed her eyes.

Diary, I could not believe she had said that. Suddenly I was almost more frightened than the morning we found out that Papa was in the gaol. I was certain that Mama's wits were wandering.

"Mama, we have no money for a maid." The words just flew out of my mouth.

Mama sat up. She said, "I must have a maid, Arabella. Your wretched father — " She began to cry. She went into such a fit I had to find her vinaigrette (of course she had not forgotten to bring that). I longed for Sophie. Sophie always knows what to do — and she knows how to make tea.

After Mama had calmed a bit, she started all over again about the maid. Diary, I do not know what to do about shopping or cooking or going to school or finding Charlie or helping Papa or — or about anything else in the world, but I do know we are NOT going to get a maid.

Mama began crying and wringing her hands again. Then she said, "Arabella, I cannot go on without a maid. You will have to ask Mr. Dewhurst for the money. Mrs. Dewhurst will help you locate someone. Arabella, you know I cannot manage without. You know that."

Diary, I was so angry I wanted to strike her. I wanted to strike my own mother. I have never felt that way before. Never in my whole life. I had to leave her. I came into this room and closed the door and here I am, sitting on the bed, writing to you. I have got over my fright. I do not really believe that Mama's wits are wandering. I believe she just refuses to understand how desperate we are. I can but pray she will understand better in the morning.

Oh, I wish Charlie were here!

Wednesday night, 21 February
Harvard House

Dear Diary,

Yes, I know, I have not written you a single word in a whole month. Until this very moment I have not had even the bittiest scrap of time when I have not fallen asleep before I could even open your pretty blue cover.

Do you wonder what the address at the top of this page means? Do you wonder where I am sitting? Please be patient, I shall tell you everything. There is so much to tell, I scarcely know where to begin, but you know how I like to have things orderly, so I shall begin where I left off.

To my mind this is a tale that ought to have a title. So I am giving it one.

<u>THE LAST WORST THING THAT HAS HAPPENED TO ME</u>

No more tonight. I am too tired.

Dear Diary,

Here beginneth my tale of <u>The Last Worst Thing that Has Happened to Me.</u>

Neither Mama nor I ate supper that night in King Street nor did we see each other. The next morning Mama got up. She dressed herself and went out. (I do not believe that Mama had ever dressed herself before in her entire life.) When she returned, she came into my room. I was sitting on the bed. This is what we said and what we did.

Mama did not look at me. She said, "Arabella, I have had to sell my mother's emerald brooch to Mr. Burke and I have engaged a young person to be my maid. She will arrive here after dinner."

For a moment my mind stopped the way a clock does when it is not wound — one tick, then nothing. Then the thoughts began shoving and jumping all over each other. "What do you mean, Mama? What will she do? Where will she sleep? Where will I?"

Mama said, "She will have to sleep in this room."

"But Mama, where am I to sleep?"

"Arabella, I cannot think of everything. Your father — " Mama began to wring her hands. (You might think she would wear them out!) "I am writing to my cousin in England for passage money home for us. My family will take care of us. Arabella, I must lie down.

You will have to bring me a cup of tea. I cannot — "

She drifted away without saying anything more. Those are the only words I can think of to describe how Mama left that room. She simply drifted away into her bedroom.

I did not know what to do. I was so frightened. Mama wished us to go to England. I could not think about that. All I could think was that I might have to work in a factory and eat in a soup kitchen, or starve to death on the street. All the time Mr. D. was helping us sell our house and belongings, I was feeling so wretched about Jane and Patty and all the girls at school knowing about it, worrying about how we would manage, worrying about Papa and Charlie, but never, ever did I think that Mama would cast me out. How can a mother cast out her own child?

I know Mama has always preferred Charlie but I have thought that she cared about me, too. She does not. She does not care any more about me than she does about servants. Not as much. She gave the maid my bed.

Friday night, 23 February

Dear Diary,

Here is the story continued. I was too tired to write more last night.

I did not set a foot outside my room on that day

until the afternoon when the maid came, just as Mama had said she would. The moment I saw her scared-looking face appear above the top stair, I put on my boots and grabbed my cloak and ran. I might have remained with Mama and shared the bed with the maid (and the work, too) but my mind just stopped working and I ran.

It was as cold outside as the frozen Arctic. It was snowing hard and the wind was wild. I ran and I ran and I ran until I had no breath left in me and night was falling. When I stopped, I discovered that I had come to the back of our own house. I suppose I was like a lost cat or dog, crawling back to the only place it knows. I crept up to our back door. The new people must not have moved in for the house was completely dark. The door was locked. I did not go around to see if the front door was unlocked. I was so weary, so hungry, so cold and so unhappy that I was quite willing to freeze to death.

I almost did. The snow was that sharp stinging kind of snow that finds its way around the edges of one's clothes and down into one's boots. And the wind was howling like a pack of wolves. I crouched up against the door and I must have been more than half asleep when I heard a cry. Something pushed against me. At first I thought I was having a dream but it pushed again and cried louder. I came fully awake. It was Dolly.

Dolly was meant to be in Belleville with Sophie. Later I figured out that she must have hidden herself at moving time, but when I was freezing by our back door I did not think, I just hugged and hugged that best cat in all the world until she squawked like a chicken. I almost fell asleep a few times more during that horrible night but Dolly would push against me and I always woke up. You know, Diary, people say that if you fall asleep out in the cold and snow you will freeze to death. Well, I did not freeze to death and it is because of Dolly. I do not care what anyone may say, cats understand so much! My little grey Dolly, my dear, sweet, wonderful Dolly kept me alive all that night. Even though I do not love my life very much now, I do not want to be dead.

I am too tired to write more.

Saturday night, 24 February

Dear Diary,

<u>The Last Worst Thing that Has Happened to Me</u> (continued again):

As soon as there was the thinnest line of light in the sky, I got up from the step. My cloak is warm enough for a brisk walk but it is not warm enough for sleeping in all night in the bitter winter cold. And boots are not warm at all — especially when they have snow inside them. I was as cold as those snow people

Charlie and Patty and I used to make in the garden and I was so stiff I almost could not stand up.

I still did not know what to do but I HAD to do something and Dolly was winding herself around and around my feet, as she always does when she is hungry. We could not get into the kitchen (besides which, there was nothing there to eat). For about one half-second I thought of going back to Mama. Then I did what Sophie told me to do back before we moved. I went to Mr. Dewhurst (and Mrs. D.). It was not far to their house but it took me a long time because my feet were so cold I could scarcely walk on them and Dolly yowled to be carried. I could not refuse her when she had saved my life so I carried her and she was very heavy.

Sunday, 25 February

Dear Diary,

I wish I could tell you about coming to Harvard House all at one time but I am too tired at the end of each day. Today I have the toothache but I am determined to write. Here is more of my tale.

Mrs. D. looked horrified when she saw me at her front door. She grabbed my hand and started clucking. She said, "Oh, child, whatever has happened? Where have you been? Come inside. Come inside at once. You will surely have pneumonia!"

She pulled me into the house and up the stairs and right into her own bedroom. She clucked and sighed (Mrs. D. sighs, too) and she said that she did not wish to hear a word about what had happened until after I had a hot bath, a meal and a rest. Jenny and Anne and all the small children were crowding around. Mrs. D. sent some of them to the kitchen with Dolly and kept shooing the rest of them away but they paid her no mind. I did not care whether they were there or not except that Jenny never stopped asking questions — but, at last, Mrs. D. sent her off with the little ones to ask Cook to make my breakfast and feed Dolly.

I had the bath — in Mrs. D's own bedroom before the fire — and it felt so wonderful that I did not ever want to get out. But I had to and, when I was completely dry and dressed in one of Anne's nightgowns, Mrs. D. had the cook bring my breakfast. I could have swooned when the odour of frying ham came sailing up the stairs. I felt so much better for that breakfast (which I ate from a tray in Mrs. D.'s bed) that I almost did not want to sleep. There was buttered porridge and there were thick slices of absolutely-perfect ham. There were scones with strawberry preserve that Mrs. D. had made in the summer. And hot tea! It was the best breakfast I have ever had in my whole, entire life!

Dear Diary,

I fell asleep again last night. Forgive me.

I slept all that day at the Dewhursts' house. When I woke up, I went to the window and looked out. The snow had stopped and there was no wind. The sky was black as ink and filled to the brim with millions of stars. Everything seemed so peaceful that I felt peaceful, too. A. came and found me one of her warm wool dresses. It was a dark red colour with blue trim and it was only a bit too big. We went downstairs together. (I like A. and J. I wish we might be friends but I can see that it will not do now.)

The dining room had a cheery fire crackling away in the fireplace and supper was every bit as good as breakfast. (Anne told me it was a special supper because of my being there.) We ate boiled beef with carrots and potatoes and a plum cake for afterwards — but, Diary, you cannot imagine all the noise at that table. The whole family was there and everyone talked at the same time. I think I told you that there are eight D. children and A. is the oldest. The youngest is only a bit past one year and, while I am not meant to notice such things, I believe Mrs. D. is soon to have another one. Mr. D. sat back and took no notice of the children and Mrs. D dithered and clucked. I think a family of monkeys in Hindustan must be something like the D. family but they are jolly and I felt warm and safe with them.

After supper, Mr. and Mrs. D. sent A. and J. off to the nursery with the children (they have no nursemaid) and asked me to go into the parlour with them to tell them what had happened. I own I was a bit ashamed afterwards that I had told them what Mama had done. Mr. D. cleared his throat. Then he said, "Arabella, you must make peace with your mother."

Mrs. D. took my hand. She said she knew Mama was vexing but that I should do my best to understand and to forgive her. I asked her, "Could you forgive your mother if she had given your bed to a servant girl?" I could not help myself.

She said she would find it difficult but that I was to remember that God "enjoined us to forgive one another." I said I would try. But, Diary, truly I fear I shall never, ever be able to forgive Mama.

Mr. D. said that, if I really felt that I could not bring myself to return to Mama, much as it grieved him, the only thing he could see for me to do was to seek employment. I was terrified that he meant work in one of those terrible factories or Mr. Marian's bakery because it is just down the street from the rooms where Mama is. He did not. He meant work as a house servant. He said, if I would be agreeable, he would ask Papa's permission to seek employment for me.

I said I was agreeable but then I said that I did not wish him to talk to Papa about it. Diary, I am so confused about Papa. Sometimes I am almost angry with him but, most of the time, I just feel so sad that he is in that horrible gaol. I do not wish him to know that I am working as a servant and am not living in the rooms with Mama. I told Mr. D. that. He said that he felt Papa should know. I begged and begged and I fear I may have argued a bit impertinently. I told him what Papa had said in his letter to Mama about Mr. D. taking care of us. At last, he agreed not to tell Papa. A few days later he found me this place.

Wednesday night, 28 February

Dear Diary,

It has been two days since I last wrote and I am sorry. Here, I hope, is the absolutely, positively last of the woeful tale of how I came to be at Harvard House.

I did not get pneumonia from being out all that night in the cold. I almost wish I had got it. I might have died — and I do not think that anybody on this earth would have minded. But I did not even catch cold. I think I must be one of the strongest people in Upper Canada, possibly in all of British North America.

I remained with the D.s for three days. I longed for them to invite me to live with them, but of course I knew that could not be. They have too many children as it is. What is more, why would they want me when even my own mother does not?

The miserable truth is that the work Mr. D. found is as a scullery maid in the house where Charlie's dreadful friend Jesse Harvard and his sister Elizabeth live. (E. is one of my erstwhile classmates and it is absolutely mortifying to be working as a servant in her house.) I am taking the place of the scullery maid who died last month from pneumonia. It is unbelievably horrible work and I have to wear a coarse grey dress that does not fit me (it belonged to the dead girl who must have been fatter and taller than I), with an apron over it and my hair pinned up under a mobcap, and there is so much more to the work than I could ever have believed possible.

I sleep in a cold little room in the attic over the kitchen and share a cold lumpy bed with Sukey, the housemaid. It is late at night now and I am sitting on the top step of the attic stairs just outside the bedroom door where I sit every night to write to you. I am freezing cold and my candle is nearly burned out. I shall write again as soon as I can manage to.

Post scriptum: One good thing. Dolly is to remain at the Dewhurst house. Jenny told me she would look after her.

Thursday, 1 March (at the top of the attic stairs)

Dear Diary,

I own I was never in the scullery at home and, what is more, we did not have a scullery maid. I suppose Sophie did all this work herself. The scullery is not cheerful like the kitchen. It is a small, cold, grey room with a stone floor and a big wooden sink lined with lead where I must clean vegetables and wash dishes and pots. The window is small and it is too high up for me to be able to see outside. The scullery always smells of lye soap and old vegetables. It is dreary and the work is so very hard.

This is what I must do each day.

1. See to it that the fire is going in the big stove in the kitchen and in the fireplace in the servants' hall by six o'clock in the morning, fill the kettle from the pail in the scullery and set it over the kitchen fire. (I have never been able to start a fire so you can imagine how cross Cook has been with my poor efforts.)

2. Make the morning tea for the "upper servants" — Sukey and Joe and I have our tea when the others have finished theirs. I have never made tea before now, either, but it is easier than starting a fire. It is really only a matter of remembering how many spoonfuls of tea are to go into the pot.

3. Scrub the floors in the kitchen, scullery and pantries, scrub all the cupboards and dressers in the

kitchen, pantries and scullery, and may heaven help me if a single ant or cockroach is to be found when I have finished. Or mouse. OR RAT! I am sure there would be a cat here if Cook were not afraid of them. Imagine being afraid of cats! My Dolly could keep this entire house free of rats and mice.

4. Set the breakfast table in the servants' hall, then clear it after breakfast (to be precise, after the morning prayers).

5. Wash the dishes from the servants' breakfast. Cook washes the family's china dishes. I am not allowed to touch them for fear I might break one. I must wash ALL the pots from the family's AND the servants' meals and you can have no suspicion of how black and greasy pots can get and how hard one must scrub with horrid washing soda and soap when the water goes cold.

6. Collect the eggs from the hen yard. (Of course there is no collecting eggs from the hens in this season so I must go down into the dark cellar and get them out of the fat where they are stored and I am terrified of the cellar. I am sure there are rats there — and maybe snakes. Charlie told me once that there are always snakes in cellars — I never, ever went into ours at home.)

Diary, merely writing this list wearies me. All the days are the same. I scrub the pots, the sink, the floors, cupboards and dressers. I peel and scrub vegetables then take the peelings — and the rotted vegetables out to the heap in the garden (if you have never smelled a potato when it has rotted, you cannot know how bad a smell can be).

I am not finished for the day until the last of the pots are put away. This is always after nine o'clock at night. It is drudgery. Drudgery! DRUDGERY! And I am SO tired. Diary, I never, ever knew a person could be this tired. My feet are tired. My back is tired. My knees are tired. My hands are red and sore from the soap and washing soda.

Worse than everything else, in fact, the worst possible chore in all the world is that I must empty the chamber pots of all the female servants into the privy out back and clean them with vinegar. (Oh, Diary, this is such a terrible thing to have to do that I am sure God will forgive forever every sin I have ever committed — or ever might commit.)

There is one other thing that is almost worse than chamber pots — well, worse in a different way. Cook told me the morning after I came here that she thinks Arabella is much too fancy a name for a scullery girl and that she will call me Betty because that was the last scullery girl's name (the dead one). I wish Betty Marvell could know this. She would not think it at all amusing. Diary, if I were a boy, I would have run away. This is what I have finally come to think must be what my brother did. It is exactly like him to have done so! Oh, why did he not think to take me with him?

Friday night, 2 March

Dear Diary,

I am sitting at the top of the attic stairs again with my shawl tight around me and my shoes on my feet because it is VERY cold. I just heard the clock in the front hall strike ten. I could not find a single minute to write to you all day until now.

Diary, I would have been much, much friendlier to Peggy at home if I had known how hard being a servant is. I wonder where she is now. I wonder where Mary is, and Sophie. Especially Sophie. I miss her so much. I do believe she was my only friend in all the world — she was certainly a better friend than Patty or Jane. Much better! I can see now that both Patty and Jane were not really friends at all. Neither one of them came to see me after Papa went to gaol, not once, nor wrote a single word to me (not after the note Patty gave me in school). Sophie would write to me, if she knew where I was. I wonder what she would say if she knew I was scrubbing vegetables and floors for the cook in Elizabeth Harvard's house — and must be someone called Betty.

Oh, Diary, I am unjust! How could I have said that Sophie was my only friend? You are my friend and Mr. and Mrs. D. and the D. children are kind and they are keeping Dolly. (I would certainly not be allowed to have her here so I must be glad — but I do miss her terribly.) Jenny has written me a note. She and Anne have invited me to visit them but, now that I have become a servant girl, of course it will not do. But it WAS good of them to invite me.

Mr. D. looked very sad when he told me about this position. He said that he wished that he could have found me something better but, as I had "no employment experience," this was the best he could do. He told me that Mr. Harvard was a fair-minded man, said to be kind to his servants (but Mr. H. does not know about Cook and Sukey and Joe). I hate, hate, hate this work but I am so afraid that if I did not have it, I would have to work in one of those factories or live in the asylum or, even worse, beg in the street. So I suppose I had better be grateful. But I do not feel grateful. Not one bit!

Before I came here, Mrs. D. went with me to King Street to get my clothes and my books. Mama was in her room. She told the maid to tell us that she was not feeling able to see us. To tell the truth, I was not sorry. I did not wish to see Mama. I only wished to gather my clothes and my books. I gathered up my clothes and my little doll and Charlie's owl but I could not find any of the books. I looked everywhere, but they had disappeared — every one of them. For a moment I was in a panic because I could not find you, either. You were on the floor, way under the bed. (I think an angel was keeping you safe). I asked the maid (her name is Maggie) about the books. She said that she had taken them to Mama, who told her to sell them. Oh, Diary, my books! How could Mama be so cruel? How could she?

Saturday night, 3 March

Dear Diary,

I am back at the top of the stairs again late at night. It is not comfortable and I am very tired but I have no other place or time to write on your pages unless I wait until tomorrow. (That is not true. If I manage to have everything washed and dried and put away after dinner and have no errands to run, I am free until it is time to set the table for tea in the servants' hall, but I always fall asleep on the stool in the scullery — and wake with my head flopped over the sink.)

We have every second Sunday afternoon free, from dinner to tea, and, every second month, we have Wednesday afternoons. (My first Wednesday afternoon will not be until March fourteenth.) Mr. Dewhurst wrote a contract with Mr. H. and these times away from work are written into it. (Sometimes scullery girls do not get the every-second-month Wednesdays.) Also that I am to be paid five pounds in a year, half in June, half in December.

Sunday afternoon, 4 March (sitting on my bed)

Dear Diary,

Today is Sunday and we went to church. The Harvard family goes to St. James and all the servants are expected to go there, too — except Cook and Sukey who are Romans. Diary, it is truly dreadful. Servants and paupers and soldiers do not sit in the pews. ~~They~~ We must sit on the benches around the edges of the church. So there I sit where all the girls from school can see me. I know that Patty saw me today because, when I looked up towards the gallery, she turned away quickly and never looked my way again. I felt so hurt and so humiliated that I could not like the singing or follow a word of the prayers. (My prayer book is wherever all my other books have gone.) I kept my head down and did not look at anyone but I did pray for Papa — and for Charlie. I cannot bear church now — and I do NOT believe Dr. Strachan cares a twig about poor people.

Monday night, 5 March

Dear Diary,

Tonight I mean to tell you something about this house.

First of all, it is bigger and finer than our house (our one-time house, to be precise) but not as big or as fine as Mr. Boulton's Grange. It has a beautiful big front door, painted shiny black, with a white-painted pillar on either side of it. It has more land around it than we had and its tall iron fence has a very handsome gate.

It is in Lot Street, the same street as ours but farther west. When I run errands for Cook, sometimes I must pass our old house and sometimes I see neighbours who used to call on Mama. They turn their heads away but, what makes me almost laugh, even when I am feeling so crushed, is that their dogs all come running to greet me with barks and yips and much jumping about. I think this says something about the kindheartedness of dogs. Yesterday, I think Mr. Boulton's little terrier, Angus, would have come ~~home~~ back to the Harvards' house with me had I allowed him to.

The only part of this house's inside I know is the basement, the servants' part. The door to the basement is on the east side of the house, just in front of the gate into the kitchen garden. (The coach house and stables are on the other side of the garden.) Inside the door there is an entryway. From here, one can go into the kitchen through one door, go into the scullery and the larder through another door, go up one set of stairs to the servants' bedchambers or go up another set to the back of the family's part of the house. It is really quite confusing when one is a stranger.

The kitchen is big and square. The stove is a big, black one like Sophie's. It stands along the back wall. This house is older than ours so there is still a fireplace and the stove is set partway into it. The big wooden table is in the centre of the room. Two other walls are covered with huge open dressers that hold dishes and pots (although some pots hang from the ceiling both in the kitchen and the scullery).

The dumbwaiter is beside the scullery door. (When I was small, I used to crawl into the dumbwaiter at home, but I cannot believe Elizabeth or Charlotte Harvard would ever dare do that with Cook in charge.) Sukey has to put the meals on the dumbwaiter shelves, then run to the upstairs pantry and pull them up. She complains and complains, but I expect she would complain a lot more if she had to carry all those dishes, one by one, up the stairs — or even on trays. But Sukey complains about absolutely everything, anyway.

The front kitchen wall has the door that leads to the servants' hall. (I was never in the servants' hall at home.) It is really a dining room with a long table that takes up almost the whole room. There is a big dresser full of dishes on one wall in this room, too. Beside it is the row of bells connected to all the rooms upstairs. (You should see everyone leap up when one of those bells jingles!) The fireplace is on the other wall. I think it would be a pleasant room if the people around the table were friendlier. I must say the same for the kitchen.

Tuesday night, 6 March

Dear Diary,

I will confess to you that I have been feeling very sorry for myself. This afternoon I could hear girls' voices in the breakfast parlour. Sukey told me, when she came to bed tonight, that one of "Miss Elizabeth's friends" wanted to come down to the kitchen to watch me working in the scullery but Miss E. would not allow it. Sukey thought it was funny.

I have now, as Tim the coachman says, "got a better grip on" myself and I am going to not think about that. I am going to tell you about the people in this house.

The family members are: Mr. Harvard, Mrs. Harvard, Jesse (you know about him!), Elizabeth, Charlotte, who is six years old, and Mrs. Parliament, who is Mrs. Harvard's mother. I have never seen Mrs. P. She lives in rooms at the back of the house above the breakfast parlour.

Oh, I almost forgot, there is one other. He is Hector, a little brown and white dog. I think he is some kind of spaniel. He belongs to Mrs. P. and Cook does not like him. But she is obliged to feed him. Joe takes him walking.

The servants are: Mr. Banks, the butler, Mrs. Evans, the housekeeper, Mrs. Muldoon, the cook (who is not at all like Sophie, she is tall and thin and has reddy-grey hair and is NOT comfortable), Alice Foster, little Charlotte's nursemaid, Sukey, the house-maid (who is NOT nice), Tim, the groom and coach-man (the Harvards have two horses, a sleigh, their own coach and a gig), Joe, the footman who is from England and talks like Mr. Jenkins (but is NOT as agreeable!).

Mr. Harvard is a stern-looking man. He comes from Scotland. He is tall and thin with thick grey hair and a bushy grey beard. He is in the Bank of Upper Canada. He has a very deep voice. He leads the prayers we must all attend in the big front hall for at least an hour every morning — and sometimes, when I am in the scullery, I can hear his voice rumbling through the ceiling from the breakfast parlour. I think he smokes cigars because, when I am near him, I can smell them. The smell of those cigars makes me think of Papa and then I am sad.

Mrs. Harvard is a short, stout, quiet woman and she has a soft, quiet voice but I think she is the ruler of this kingdom.

Most in the family are not unkind to me. I do not see Mr. or Mrs. H. except at prayers every morning. Elizabeth does not turn her head away when she sees me but she does not speak. She just nods and I can see that she is as uncomfortable as I. I am quite sure she does her best not to be where she might find me (which is not difficult as she has no reason to be anywhere near the scullery). I almost never see little Charlotte.

Jesse is unkind. He is more than unkind, he is horrid. The first week I was here, he came clattering into the kitchen after breakfast one morning and shoved me so that I spilled tea all over my apron from the cups I was carrying. Then he pulled my cap down over my eyes. Then he pulled on my ear and he hissed — loudly, right into my ear, "See what happens to dirty rebels' daughters, not-so-standoffish-now Miss Arabella Stevenson."

Cook told him to, "Get along Master Jesse and not bother the scullery girl, she has work to do." She told me to get about my business. Jesse whispered that I, too, must call him Master Jesse. Then he laughed and went off upstairs. (J.'s laugh reminds me of Granddad's horse Billy and I never liked that horse — although I am uneasy with horses, in any case.) It is true. I am expected to call him Master Jesse and his sisters Miss Elizabeth and Miss Charlotte. It is mortifying.

Jesse goes out of his way to torment me. He sticks his ugly head (his hair is the colour of mud) around corners just to frighten me and makes sure to tell me all the bad news from the courthouse where the rebels' trials are going on. Even though he was Charlie's friend, I never liked Jesse Harvard after he tried to kiss me at Louisa Morrison's birthday party two years ago. Now I really hate him. I hate his croaky voice. I hate his big ugly mouth. I hate everything about him. And I was never standoffish. Never! Oh, how I hope he soon tires of tormenting me!

Wednesday night, 7 March

Dear Diary,

I am at the top of the attic stairs again — I have decided to think of this as a castle tower and myself to be like Rapunzel — except that my hair most certainly is not golden!

I think I will sleep right here all night because I do not wish to be ill. Sukey has the fever and chills and a dreadful cough. Alice Foster has it, too. Mrs. Evans has got out *The Domestic Physician* (Sophie had that book, too) and has been directing Cook to dose them with sulphur and brown sugar and willow-bark tea, and rub their chests with goose grease and turpentine. (I hate that!)

At supper, everyone was talking about the rebels' trials. They have been going on at the courthouse for some time. I am always desperate for news but Mr. Banks never leaves his newspaper where I might find it. All I know is what Mr. B. tells us. He says that he fears "that some of those villainous rebels will be set free and create utter chaos." He is sure that some will be hanged and the others will all be sent to that island near Australia. It is called Van Dieman's Land and it is a prison colony like Australia where the prisoners must do horrible, back-breaking work. I cannot bear to listen to him talk like that, but I dare not let anyone see how I feel. Oh, Diary, I am so afraid for Papa!

Thursday, 8 March (on my castle tower steps)

Dear Diary,

I am NOT going to think about the trials tonight. Cook and Mr. Banks were talking about them again at supper and Sukey (she is recovered from the fever and is her usual ill-natured self) and Joe kept whispering and glancing towards me but I paid them no attention. I attended my chicken pie (even though I do not like Cook, I must admit that she is a very good cook).

I think I am slowly becoming accustomed to the work — no, no, NO, NO! That is NOT true! I do not believe that I shall EVER become accustomed to this work. I am so tired every night that I sometimes drop into bed like a great stone with hardly the strength to say my prayers. Our room has neither a stove nor a fireplace and there is always frost on the inside of the tiny window (which has no curtain).

There is no carpet on the floor and the only furniture is the bed and a small dresser which I must share with Sukey. The bed has a thin, lumpy mattress filled with straw and two worn coverlets that could not keep a housefly warm. Need I tell you there are no bed warmers for scullery maids.

So I have come to be almost grateful for Sukey because she is warm, even though she does not like me. She is two years older than I, she is a good bit taller and might be pretty if she could wash her hair and have pretty clothes. Nothing would make her agreeable, however. She is mean-minded and she has a tongue that could cut diamonds (I heard Papa say that once about Mrs. Milroy) — and she talks through her nose.

Diary, I am very lonely.

Saturday night, 10 March (on my tower steps)

Dear Diary,

Sukey is more than ill-natured. She is a truly dreadful person. You have not had a word from me for two days because she hid you. I am glad that she is a girl with no imagination because I found you straightaway. You were under the mattress of our bed (and I did not even notice the new lump).

Of course I did not begin to look for you on Thursday until after Sukey was asleep. I thought I must have forgotten where I put you — and you can imagine how that distressed me. I have a good memory but I was not feeling well because I had a little of the fever that Sukey had.

When I could not find you again last night, I scarcely slept for worrying. Then, this morning I suspected Sukey because she was forever giving me looks like the ones Maud Adams in school always gave the rest of us when she knew something we did not know.

I did not say a word to her, I just searched. The first place I looked was under our mattress and there you were. I still said nothing but I shall find my own hiding places from now on. I hope and hope and hope that Sukey did not read any of your pages.

Diary, I do not understand why she dislikes me so much. I do not really like her, either (how could I after she did such a hateful thing?) but I am not beastly to her. She puts her nose up as though she were the Queen when she sees me carrying our chamber pot — and she has to carry the ones from the "ladies of the family." When I said good morning to Joe this morning, she asked me if I was "making up to him." Can you believe she really thought that? She makes fun of me all the time. She mocks the way I talk, she laughs every time I make a mistake and she sets out to make trouble for me.

Last week she stole a tea cake and some preserve

and swore to Cook that it was I. At supper that night Cook gave me no dessert. Yesterday I carefully scrubbed every single potato and carrot and turnip for both the family's dinner and the servants' dinner. Then I had to peel all the potatoes and the turnip and scrape all the carrots when Sukey told me that was how they had to be done. The next day she saw me throw out the water the carrots had been cooking in when she knew Cook always saved it for soup. Then she let Mrs. Parliament's dog out and told Cook it was I who did it. So it was I who had to go out to find him (and it was raining like Niagara Falls outside — which is how I got the fever).

Sukey is not the only one who dislikes me. I think perhaps all the servants do. Joe, who is nutty over Sukey, laughs every time she laughs and he laughs so hard I sometimes think his insides are going to fall right out of his mouth. Cook says I must call her Mrs. Muldoon while the others all call her Cook, except for Mr. Banks who calls her by her Christian name, which is Mattie. (I will not write Mrs. Muldoon on these pages, she shall be COOK.) She calls me "an uppity madam" because of my "fancy words." She means that I speak proper English and you know I cannot help that.

Mr. Banks and Mrs. Evans and Alice Foster and Tim do not laugh at me. Mr. Banks and Mrs. Evans are what Jesse Harvard calls me, standoffish. Alice

Foster is VERY retiring. Tim is too good-natured to make fun of anyone.

Diary, it is all so very dreadful — and strange. I feel a bit as though I have become detached from myself and am living someone else's life. (Well, I expect I am, I am living Betty's life.) Only last year the world was as it ought to be. Then along came Cousin Matthews and his friends, and Papa listened to them and he — oh, Diary, I lie awake at night, after Sukey is snoring (yes, she snores), no matter how tired I am, and I think about Charlie and about Papa. I long to know where Charlie is and if he is well. And Papa. Oh, Diary, I ache to see him and hug him. And ask him questions, questions, questions! Then, sometimes — oh, I know I should not write this even to you, but I shall — sometimes I feel so angry that I think I do not ever wish to see Papa again, not even should he be freed from the gaol tomorrow morning and come to take me away from here.

Sunday, 11 March (on my tower steps)

Dear Diary,

This afternoon was my first Sunday afternoon away from this house. The weather was inclement on my first Sunday. I had the toothache and did not go out. Today I went to see Mama. Truly, I do not know why I did that. She was lying on her chaise longue.

She said not a word of greeting. She complained about not being able to bathe properly, she complained about the terrible food, she complained that the maid was slow and stupid. (I am sure Maggie could hear her through those thin walls. I never used to think about what servants could hear through walls.) She complained about Papa. She wanted to know why Charlie did not come to see her and she did not believe that I do not know where he is. I asked her why she sold my books. She said not to bother her about "trifling matters." How can selling my books — my BOOKS — be a trifling matter? How could Mama do this? How COULD she?

Then she gave me a letter to post (she does not trust Maggie). She has written again to our relatives in England to ask them to send us passage money.

I have no money but, if I had some, I would NOT spend it on postage to England (I would buy books). I am not sure I would like England if it is full of the people Miss St. Clair and Mrs. Milroy admire so much, people like Mama. Diary, I ought not to have written that. But, truly, I do think it, so I am going to write it again, PEOPLE LIKE MAMA who cast out their own children (and sell their possessions). All the same, living in England with Mama must be better than living in the scullery.

I told Mama that I had no money and she gave me enough for the postage. You can see by that how desperately she desires to go to England. Diary, do you think Mama's relatives really will take us in?

My first Wednesday half-holiday comes in two more days. I mean to visit Mr. Jenkins. Do you remember him? He is my friend the shoemaker in Duke Street. I shall not go to Mama again. Oh, Diary, I feel such a pain in my heart that Mama does not care for me.

Good night, Diary.

Monday, 12 March (on my tower steps)

Dear Diary,

I just read what I wrote you about Papa on Saturday. Diary, I do not really mean that. I am still quite angry at him but I think I do wish to see him — and Charlie. If C. were here, I would shake him — but, then, as soon as I think that, I am afraid again. What if he did not run off? What if he is hurt somewhere and cannot get help? What if he is dead? Diary, I cannot believe that, but, then, where can he be? Why does he not send word? Why does he not come and find me and take me away from here?

Yesterday at dinner everyone was talking about the trials again. They are on and then off and then on again and no one knows what will happen. Mr. Banks says it is disgraceful that WLM "and his crowd" got off scot-free by escaping over the border, and that people say there is danger of invasion from them and their American friends.

Sometimes I wish the trials would just be over, no matter what that judge decides. Then I get really scared and pray especially hard that Papa will be set free. Then the misery floods over me again like high storm waves over the lakeshore and all I can think is that everything is so unfair. Papa ought not to have been in the rebellion. He ought not to be in that gaol. I OUGHT NOT TO BE IN THIS HOUSE!

I am so cold and so tired and so unhappy and SO DIRTY. Once a week we are permitted to bathe in a tin tub in the kitchen. And we lower female servants (Sukey and I) must SHARE the bath water. Can you credit that? I am second because I am newer and younger — and smaller — and you can only imagine what the bath water is like by the time it comes to me! It is disgusting! But, at least, Cook hangs sheets around so we do not have to bathe in sight of everyone.

Tuesday night, 13 March (on my tower steps)

Dear Diary,

It is late at night and here I am again on my tower steps with my candle. Sukey and Alice Foster are better but now Joe is sick so Cook sent me to the market for butter and cheese this morning. I was so glad to be away from the scullery and the day was so warm that I stopped in the market square to watch a pair of pigeons fighting over bits of bread and a farmer chase his pig around the well, with a lot of shouting and cursing. There were three men standing on boxes in the square, haranguing about politics. I did NOT wish to listen to them.

As soon as I had the butter and cheese, I hurried over to Duke Street to see Mr. Jenkins but he was not there. His shop was completely closed. I went into the watchmaker's shop next door to ask about him but the man shooed me away as though I were a stray cat. I think the words *rebel's daughter* must show on my forehead like the mark of Cain.

I hate this city now. It is full of uncharitable watchmakers and stupid guards everywhere one looks.

On the way home, the big wheels on a farmer's dray splashed mud all over me. Then I saw the hawker who used to sell us roasted chestnuts on the way home from school. He looked at me with pity and did not try to sell me anything. Then I passed New Street where Miss St. Clair's school is and I saw Betty Marvell on the front steps.

When I got ~~home~~ back here (I will <u>NOT</u> think of this house as home), Cook gave me, as Sukey says, "the back of her tongue" for being gone so long.

Good night.

Wednesday night, 14 March (on my tower steps)

Dear Diary,

Today was my first Wednesday half-holiday. The day was colder than yesterday but it was bright and there were sparrows twittering outside my window this morning so I walked down to the lake to see if it was still frozen. There were huge chunks of ice along the shore but the lake was mostly open. There were people about and dogs and carts and horses and oxen all having a dreadful time with the muddy streets.

I walked along the shore watching the fishing boats and canoes for a while, wishing so much I could talk to my friend Mr. Jenkins but he — oh! What a dunce I am!! I have just realized about Mr. Jenkins. Last summer, when I went to ask him about the Family Compact, he talked about how hard life was for ordinary people and about "drastic measures" to make our province right. He told me how wonderful WLM was. He talked just like Cousin Matthews and Mr. Bowerman, and now I see that he must have been with the rebels. So I suppose he is in the gaol or has fled into the United States. Or it may be that he is dead. Oh, Diary, I do hope he is safe.

Thursday night, 15 March

Dear Diary,

I woke in the middle of the night last night. It was raining and the wind was rattling the windowpane and driving the rain through the cracks in the wall. I could not get back to sleep so I got out of bed (my half a bed, to be precise) and went out onto the landing to write to you again — but I did not write. I sat, shivering in my shawl in the flickering light of my candle stub (really it was Sukey's candle stub).

The truth is, Diary, that I was feeling VERY sorry for myself. I was so deep in misery that I did not realize for quite some time that I was smelling coffee. When I did realize it, it took me another minute or two to think how odd it was for someone to be brewing coffee so late at night.

You know how inquisitive I am. I HAD to discover who it was. So I crept down the stairs and listened at the kitchen door. I could not hear anything. I peered through the keyhole but I could not see anyone. I opened the door a crack and still I could not see anyone. I slipped into the room. There was no one there and the coffee pot was not on the stove, but the room was filled with the smell of coffee. It was midnight. I heard the tallcase clock up in the big front hall strike twelve just as I went into the room.

What a mystery it is! Can you imagine the to-do

there will be if Cook finds out that someone has been in her kitchen brewing coffee in the middle of the night? (Unless it was Mr. Banks or Mrs. Evans, but that is unlikely, they are both too proper.) Who could it be? Who would dare? Diary, it gives me the shivers to think about it, but what a mystery!

The kitchen was warm and quiet and it was SO comfortable without Cook there (or anyone) that I sat down in Cook's rocking chair by the stove and snuggled into my shawl. I knew I was being bold and I was as nervous as a kitten but I put my feet right on the little ledge under the oven and sat there for the longest time.

And I am in that very same place tonight, at this very moment, in Cook's chair by the fire.

Later

I have not written one word for almost an hour. I have been sitting and rocking, looking at the reflection of the last of the firelight on the dishes on the dresser shelves, and listening to the creak of the chair rockers on the wooden floor. I feel so comfortable in the warm, quiet kitchen that thoughts have been drifting around and around in my head until I have come to understand something. I have come to understand that I have not really become someone named Betty. I am still Arabella. I cannot be Betty, I do not know how to be Betty. (I wonder if Betty was the dead girl's own name or if it belonged to someone who died before she came here.)

Once last year I went to the theatre with Mama to see a play. (It was *The Lady of the Lake* and it was very beautiful!) If I could act like the actors in that play, I could act Betty for Cook and Sukey and Joe and Mr. Banks and everyone, but I do not believe I can do that. So they may call me Betty all day long — Betty, Betty, Betty — but I am not going to pretend to be that person. Even though I have to wear this mob-cap and these horrid grey dresses and aprons. Even though they laugh at me and call me madam. Even though I have never much liked my names (well, not the first two), I am still myself, Arabella Eleanora Stevenson. And, AND even should Mama's relatives in England not have us, I mean to get my own life back. All of it. Every bit. I do not know how but I WILL do it. Somehow!

I felt so much better after I made that decision, Diary, that I got up and went to the drawer in the kitchen table and pulled out the little sharp knife no one is to touch but Cook (she even washes it herself) and I sharpened this bit of pencil with it. I put the shavings in the stove. Then I wrote those thoughts.

Dear Diary,

I felt so peaceful after I wrote to you last night, that I fell asleep in Cook's chair and dreamed of Dolly. (Do you remember that she is living with the Dewhurst family now?) Her mewing was so loud it woke me. I went upstairs to bed and I still felt better about the world when I got up this morning.

Then the world turned upside down again. I am in the scullery (I hid you under the stepping stool) and I must write this quickly because I shall be in such trouble if I am discovered. I DID smell coffee Wednesday night and Cook has accused me of brewing it. (I do not know how she found out about it.) There was nothing I could say to defend myself, but I tried. That made her so angry that she shook me and slapped my face. Diary, no one has ever slapped my face. Not in my whole life. I felt so humiliated. But I did not cry. Not one tear. Not one.

And YOU know that I did not brew the coffee! But now I am in disgrace and may not go out on my next free Sunday. I cannot think who made that coffee because there was not a soul in the servants' hall the last two nights and no one else in the house was stirring that I could hear. It is very mysterious and I wish whoever it was would own up to the crime.

Sunday–Monday night, 18–19 March

Dear Diary,

It is the middle of the night between Sunday and Monday and I am down in the kitchen again — AND I smell coffee again. What am I to do? Am I to lose my position? Scullery work is hateful above all things but I think it must be better than having to work in a factory and live out in the street. I have seen the ragged children in the street. What happens to them? I am really frightened, Diary. I need to solve this mystery. RIGHT AWAY!!

Friday night, 23 March (in the kitchen)

Dear Diary,

The mystery is solved!

I have been in such trouble with Cook that you might think I would stop coming down to the kitchen at night. But I had to solve the mystery. And, what is more, the kitchen at night has become my one comfort — no, one of two comforts, you are the other. Also I do not believe it would make any difference if I were to stop. Cook WANTS to blame me.

I did not write on Monday or Tuesday night or even come into the kitchen because I fell asleep in bed both nights and did not wake until morning.

Wednesday night I woke up too late to catch the criminal and then I was too sleepy to write on your pages.

I resolved to come down to the kitchen earlier last night. I waited until long after Sukey began snoring — and I did not fall asleep. In fact, I waited so long I feared I might be too late. But I was not. I could smell coffee as soon as I got to the bottom of the stairs. I opened the door very slowly and very quietly, and peered inside. There was a woman just lifting the coffee pot from the stove. I was so surprised, I almost dropped my candle (even though I was hoping to see someone).

For a moment, I thought she was a ghost and I was terrified. But the smell of coffee was real and the pot was real, and I soon figured out that the woman must be real, too.

She looked old and frail and I feared that, if she were to turn and catch sight of me, I would frighten her, so I cleared my throat just the tiniest bit. All the same, she jumped — straight up like a grasshopper. She dropped the pot onto the stove with a clang and whirled about.

She was very small, almost as short as I, and thin, although I am not absolutely sure about thin, because she had on a heavy nightdress with a big, thick, brown shawl over it. She had dark slippers on her feet. She had a nightcap pulled down almost to her eyebrows but I could see that her hair was white because there was a long white plait hanging down her back. She had a thin, wrinkled face. I could not think who she might be.

Her eyes went wide (the way Dolly's do when she is upset) and she stared and stared at me. I expect she thought I was as unreal as I had thought her. I stared back. I do not know which of us was the more apprehensive but, after we had stared at each other for the longest time, I got up my courage and asked her who she was.

"I am Louisa Parliament," she said. Louisa Parliament. She is Mrs. Harvard's mother and she lives in rooms over the breakfast parlour.

She sighed. Then she said, "I ought not to be here and I presume you have been sent to tell me so. I knew I should be discovered."

I told her that I had not been sent to tell her anything. I told her I was not meant to be there, either. Mrs. Parliament giggled. Another surprise! I have never heard an adult person giggle.

She picked up the coffee pot and waved it at me. She said, "In which case, would you like a share of my contraband?"

Diary, I drank some of Mrs. Parliament's coffee. It was bitter but I liked it (it was the first coffee I have ever had). We talked. The room grew colder and colder and we did not dare add more wood to the stove so we huddled together in front of it and talked and talked and talked. Mrs. P. comes from out in the country, near where Papa grew up, and she knew Gran and Granddad a little. She shook her head and clucked her tongue and her face got sad when I told her about Papa and what had happened to us. She said that she knew about Papa. She said she would say a prayer for him and for Charlie and Mama (I did not tell her about Mama giving my room to Maggie, the maid).

We washed the coffee pot and the cups and saucers in the scullery, then she asked me if I thought she was creating trouble for me by making the coffee. She said, "I do so love a cup of coffee, but my daughter believes it is not good for me."

She has been sneaking down to the kitchen and making it for herself to drink up in her rooms. She giggled again when she told me that. Diary, when Mrs. Parliament giggles, her mouth turns up and her eyes crinkle and it sounds just like the water running over the stones in the creek behind Gran and Grand-dad's farmhouse. I wished I could hug her. I could not tell her that I was being blamed for making the coffee.

She found out, though. This morning, Cook went to Mrs. H. to say that I would have to be dismissed because I was a thief. Mrs. H. told Mr. H. at break-fast and Mrs. P. was there. She confessed to being the coffee thief AND she did not tell Mr. and Mrs. H. OR Cook that I was in the kitchen with her. Mrs. P. came down to the kitchen a little while ago especially to tell me (but she would not stay to make coffee). Now I know why Cook has been so hateful to me all day. And all day I was waiting and waiting to have her tell me I was to be dismissed. I do not believe Cook was pleased. I believe that she would very much like to have me dismissed. This is not heartwarming.

Sunday, 25 March (late at night in the kitchen)

Dear Diary,

This is the first chance in two days that I have had to write a single word on your pages. Cook has had to give me back my free Sunday, but it is raining out. Sukey went out with Joe, in spite of that, so I had the bedroom to myself. I fell asleep. Cook cannot blame me for pinching the coffee (I do so love to use words I know Mama would hate!), so she has been finding mountains of extra work for me. I really believe she will pile chore upon chore until I cannot possibly do them all and then she will go to Mrs. H. and tell her I am unsatisfactory.

As well as doing my regular chores, I have had to wash all the table linens and press them with the smoothing iron. This house has a laundress who comes once a week to take away all the dirty linen but she is ill. (Or perhaps Cook told her not to come so that I would have to do this work — do you see how mistrustful I have become? I think I have good reason to be.) I am so tired and my hands are so red and have such sores on them I can barely write. I wash pots and linen and smell the lye soap in my sleep.

Cook sends me on some of the errands Joe usually does (she tells me that Tim needs Joe in the coach house), even walking Mrs. P.'s Hector, but I do not mind doing that. Hector and I have become friends, he is a clever little spaniel, quick and nimble. Besides that, the days are growing warmer. The snow is all but completely melted. The last of the ice has finally gone out of the harbour and the first steamship has come in — I heard its cannon go off when I was out with Hector. The geese are honking overhead and the sparrows are already at their nest-building in the apple tree in the kitchen garden. If the sores on my hands get worse, I may not be able to write for a few days but you know that you will not be forgotten.

Monday night, 26 March

Dear Diary,

I am sitting in Cook's rocking chair in the kitchen, writing by the light of the nub of the candle Sukey took upstairs — Cook is being so beastly I feared to ask her for a candle when I went up. I did not hear

Sukey come to bed but when I woke a few minutes ago, she was busy at her snoring. I could not keep from worrying about what will happen to me so I came downstairs. I have been thinking and thinking about all the extra work and how horrible Cook is and whether or not I will be dismissed and about Mrs. P. I have decided to do something very bold. I am going to make some coffee and take it to her.

Life here is so unbearable that work in a brickyard or tannery (even though I cannot stand the smell) or mill cannot be worse. So, in case I am to be dismissed tomorrow, I mean to see Mrs. P. one more time. She will be missing her coffee so she might be pleased to see me.

I am going to do it. Wish me luck!

Tuesday night (in the kitchen)

Dear Diary,

I have not been dismissed and I did make the coffee last night! I have watched Cook often enough — and washed out the wretched pot often enough — so I was fairly sure that I could do it. I put the pot and two cups and saucers on the small flowered tray on which Mrs. Evans sometimes takes her tea. I crept up the stairs to the breakfast parlour, as carefully as Dolly goes after a mouse, and then up the small flight of stairs to Mrs. P.'s door. She was still up — I could see a light from under her door. I knocked as loudly as I dared and prayed that she would hear me (and no one else, I did NOT wish to wake the family). After the longest time, she came to the door.

She looked truly surprised to see me. She smiled and she took me by the arm and pushed the door closed behind me.

"Well, well, well," she said — and do you know what, Diary? I think she gave a little skip. She pointed to a small, round table across the room where I could set the tray down by a lamp with a beautiful glass shade. Then she sat down on the sofa beside the table and pointed to the armchair on the other side of it. I sat down. Then I had a surprise. WHAT A SURPRISE! A cat leapt into my lap. It was Dolly. My Dolly!

Remember that I told you I heard her mewing the second night I was in the kitchen? I thought it was part of a dream but it really WAS Dolly. She must have run away from the Dewhurst house. I wonder if she went to our old home or if she knew, straightaway, that I was here. Do you think a cat would know that? I do.

What happened was that Mrs. P. heard the mewing, too. She went downstairs, let Dolly in and took her to her rooms and there she has been ever since. Cook will not let a cat into the kitchen but she cannot order Mrs. P. about as she does us servants so she gives her food for Dolly in her rooms. And, what do you think? Dolly sleeps in an old baby cradle Mrs. P.

has in her parlour. She lies there like a little queen, being waited on far more than she ever was at home even though Sophie was always good to her. I wonder that she does not have a pink velvet ribbon around her neck as Melissa Partridge's cat had at one of Melissa's Christmas parties (long ago when I was going to Christmas parties).

You do not have to guess how happy I was to see Dolly. I was in raptures — and she was, too. She licked my hands and my face over and over and over again and then curled up in my lap and purred and purred and purred. I think Mrs. P. was almost as happy as I, especially after I told her about Dolly finding me by our back door that night in the snowstorm. She called Dolly a phenomenal and truly faithful cat.

It was so like being at home, sitting in that cosy room (one wall has a bookcase FULL of books), holding a cup and saucer in my hand, with Dolly in my lap, that I had to swallow tears before I could take one sip of coffee. Then I almost laughed for thinking about an old woman and a girl, in their nightclothes in the middle of the night, drinking coffee like two fashionable ladies at an afternoon party.

We talked about cats and dogs and life in the country where Mrs. P. and Gran and Granddad once lived. Mrs. P. talked a lot about her grandchildren. She is worried about little Charlotte because C. has the cough and chills that Sukey and Alice Foster and Joe had (and I, a bit). Then she told me that Jesse and Elizabeth and Charlotte never seem to have any time to spend with her. She would like to have them visit and, what is more, she would like their help. She has lost much of her eyesight. Even though she has spectacles, she cannot see to read or write, except with a very strong magnifying glass. She said that she wished Jesse or Elizabeth would read her books and newspapers to her and write her letters for her.

I said that perhaps I could do that on my Sunday afternoons off. Then I remembered that I was sure to be dismissed in the morning because of making the coffee — but I could not tell her that. Oh, how I would love to read to Mrs. P. and write her letters in that room where Dolly lives and there are all those books and that beautiful lamp.

Mrs. P. said that it would be wonderful if I would do those tasks for her. She said that she believed our "midnight trysts" would have to end but that she would be delighted to see me regularly in her "apartment."

Then she said, "Arabella, you are a brave and a good girl." She said she knew that I was "courting trouble" by making the coffee. I really did almost cry then. I got up and took the coffee things away (and washed and dried them and put them where they belonged).

I went to bed but I did not sleep. I wish I were as brave as Mrs. P. thinks I am.

Wednesday night, 28 March

Diary, you will never, ever believe what has happened! I am to read and write for Mrs. P. and not on my free Sundays. I am to go every Wednesday afternoon beginning Wednesday next. EVERY Wednesday! This is NOT to be instead of my half-holiday every other month. On that week, I will go to Mrs. P. on the Sundays after dinner, and not the afternoonfree Sundays. I am to earn a whole pound in the year from Mrs. P. That makes six pounds altogether. Is this not wonderful?

Now I have every Wednesday afternoon to look forward to with Dolly and Mrs. P. and I need not worry every single minute of every single day that I might be dismissed. It is worth all the extra work I am sure I shall have to do for Cook!

My cup runneth over!

Saturday night, 31 March

Dear Diary,

Cook hates that I am to go to Mrs. P. on Wednesdays. So does Sukey. My "uppity ways" are much discussed, in loud whispers, in the kitchen and in the servants' hall at mealtime. Yesterday, at dinner, Joe said, "Will madam have a bit of turnip?" in a big mocking voice and everyone laughed (well, not everyone). I hate it. I have done nothing to make them dislike me so — and nothing to make the rest of the world look down on me, either. I did not join WLM's hateful rebellion. I did not send Papa to gaol. It is NOT fair!

I kept my head down and tried not to listen to what anyone said but then they began talking about Sir George Arthur, our new lieutenant-governor. (Sir Francis left on the steamship *Transit* last week, the very same day that Sir George arrived.) Mrs. Evans said that there will likely be a fête for Sir George next week at Government House and the whole Harvard family will surely go. Mr. Banks said that Sir G. was the governor of Van Dieman's Land before he came here. Mr. B. said he hoped he would be less harsh with our province than he was said to have been with those "brutish criminals." Everyone smiled because it was Mr. B.'s joke (he always strokes his moustache when he makes a joke) but I could not smile and I could not stop thinking about Van Dieman's Land — and then I could not eat one bite of Cook's walnut cake.

We are all praying for little Charlotte, who is very ill. Cook is piling the chores on me and I am very tired but I shall not write any more about hateful people.

Good night, Diary.

Monday night, 2 April

Dear Diary,

Mrs. P. and I talked about the rebel trials yesterday. It was not my free Sunday. I was scared and I knew I was being bold but I simply had to talk to her. I sneaked up to her rooms before tea. Mrs. P. did not mind.

Until today, I have not talked to anyone about the trials and I have tried not to think about them. At night when thoughts of them jump into my head, I force myself to turn from them. So is it not odd that I felt glad to talk to Mrs. P. about them? Well, not glad, precisely, but easy in my mind. Mrs. P. said that I must be brave and continue to pray hard for Papa. I confessed that I was not one bit brave and that I had not been able to force myself to visit Papa in the gaol, but that I do pray very hard. All the time.

There has not been much about the trials in Mrs. P's newspaper except that the editor does not consider either Chief Justice Robinson or Mr. Christopher Hagerman to be fair people. Diary, did I ever tell you how much Papa dislikes Mr. H.? And he is the province's attorney general. He is in charge of all the government lawyers. In fact, I do not think that editor likes those men at all. Some of the rebels have been set free — but not Papa.

This morning, Jesse Harvard came into the kitchen

garden when I was raking last fall's leaves from the beds. He was bent on telling me that Papa is sure to be hanged. J. is the most hateful boy the world has ever had in it! He said Mr. Christopher Hagerman would see to the hangings. J. says that people call him "the hungry tiger" because he means to see "every last rebel" hanged.

Diary, I am so afraid for Papa. I do not really feel angry at him anymore. I still cannot like the horrid rebellion but now I can see that those Family Compact men are VERY unfair.

Wednesday night, 4 April

Dear Diary,

Mrs. Parliament is my salvation. I believe she is my guardian angel (she looks just as an angel ought, small and shining). She is kind and she makes me laugh and she let me sit with Dolly on my lap all afternoon. We did not begin the book she wishes me to read to her. We talked about books we liked and she has let me borrow both a *Blackwood's Magazine* AND her copy of *The Pilgrim's Progress* (can you believe that I have missed that book?). After I wrote a letter to her niece in Picton, she spent all the rest of our time telling me stories about growing up on the farm. I felt a little sad because her stories made me think of all Granddad's farm stories, but she made me laugh, too.

Pigs and geese are very entertaining.

I think Mrs. P. is wise about many things but when she says I must not "fret about my circumstances," I do not see much wisdom in that. Mrs. P. says that it tells us in the Bible that we are never given a greater burden than we can bear. I certainly hope she is right because sometimes I am not at all sure — and I do NOT mean to bear this burden forever.

Little Charlotte is better. The household is rejoicing.

Friday night, 6 April

Dear Diary,

Mr. Banks said at supper that his newspaper had "informed" him that Peter Matthews and Samuel Lount, the blacksmith from the Holland Marsh, are sentenced to be hanged for treason next week (Diary, my skin went cold when he told us that). Cook said she thought every last rebel should be hanged (and she looked right at me when she said it). I think everyone agreed with her except Mrs. Evans (and perhaps Alice Foster). Mrs. E. said she considered "that remark to be a trifle bloodthirsty."

I needed to talk to Mrs. P. so I sneaked up to her rooms to see her after I finished in the scullery (it was not much past nine o'clock). I had to ask if she thought all the rebels would be hanged. She said that she did not believe that would happen to any others. She does think they might be transported to the prison colony in Van Dieman's Land. Her newspaper says that, too.

Mrs. P. took both my hands when she said that. Then she asked me if I might not wish to try again to visit Papa.

I have been sitting here in Cook's chair for the longest time, rocking and thinking about Papa and about Van Dieman's Land. It is thousands and thousands of miles from here, near Australia in the Pacific Ocean. Sophie told me there are gigantic birds there that eat people. I think that it may not be true about the birds, but what if the man in charge of the prisoners is as harsh as Sir George Arthur?

I long to see Papa but I am dreadfully afraid of the gaol.

Monday night, 9 April

Dear Diary,

I thought about visiting Papa for two whole days but the more I thought about it, the more I did not know what to do. (I might have gone yesterday as it was my Sunday afternoon free but I could not bring myself to do it. Instead, I kept to my — our — attic room and forgot myself in Mrs. P.'s *Blackwood's Magazine*.)

Last night the thoughts began all over again. This is how I thought: I long to see Papa. But I cannot go back to that gaol. What if he is sent to that terrible island and I never see him again? But the gaol is so horrible. But what if he goes away forever? But I am so afraid of the gaol. Back and forward, my thoughts flew. Back and forward, back and forward, like shuttle-cocks.

Finally I could not bear the fight inside my head another moment, so, this afternoon, when Cook was napping in her chair, I dashed (I really did!) off to Mr. D.'s office to ask for his help. Mr. D. was as kind and polite as he had been the other time I went to his office, even though I had my horrid grey scullery dress on (and my pretty rose-coloured shawl is no longer pretty — or really even rose-coloured). He asked about my life at Harvard House. I told him about Mrs. P. and he smiled and told me he had always considered her to be a fine woman. Then he said that he would arrange for me to see Papa.

I feel very strange about this — and scared.

Tuesday afternoon, 10 April

Mr. Banks told us at dinner that two more rebels are sentenced to be hanged on April 24. One of them is Mr. John Montgomery, who owned the tavern at the Eglinton Crossroads where the battle was.

Dear Diary,

I have seen Papa. I HAVE SEEN PAPA! It was wonderful and it was horrible. I was glad and I was sad. Oh, Diary, gaol is the dreadfullest, disgustingest place in the whole world! I shall never complain again about the room I share with Sukey in the attic (even though it is not nice). Gaol is dark and cold and slimy and it smells of rotting things and privies and every bad thing one could ever imagine — and some things no one could ever imagine. And there are rats!

Poor Papa! Poor, poor Papa! He was always so neat and now he is dirty and his hair is not cut and he has a scraggly beard like the beards one sees on beggars, he smells terrible and he is so thin and so sad. He did not want to hug me because he was so dirty but, when I hugged him, he hugged and hugged me back and he wept. Diary, I could not imagine that Papa would weep. But I did not care because I wept, too.

I mean to spend my first six-months' wages, when I get them, on stationery and pens and ink and bread and cheese for Papa. (Mr. D. says Papa would like these things.)

Mr. D. sent me a note late yesterday afternoon, "through the kind offices of Mrs. Parliament," asking me to be ready at one o'clock today, when he would come for me. (Mrs. P. said she was happy to give me the afternoon to visit Papa.) He was here at precisely one o'clock in his gig. (I could not help hoping that Sukey and Cook and Joe were all watching — Jesse Harvard, too!)

I put on my good blue wool dress and my velvet bonnet so as not to let Papa know that I am working as a scullery maid. I did not take my shawl. I did not want him to see that! Now I shall have to rid myself of these clothes. (Sukey made dreadful faces and told me that I would have to "burn them stinking gaol clothes.") But I am glad I wore them because Papa thinks I am living in the rooms with Mama. When I saw how dreadful he felt about those rooms, I was gladder and gladder that he does not know about me.

We talked (after we had stopped weeping) and Papa said that he did not know what would happen to him. He said that Mr. Christopher Hagerman was "a stiff man without a drop of kindness in his blood" but that Mr. Robert Baldwin is the barrister defending the rebels and he is a good man, and that Chief Justice Robinson, who is the judge in all the trials, is a just man. (The man who writes Mrs. P.'s newspaper does not think that.) Papa said he knew that Cousin Matthews and the others are to be hanged in spite of Chief Justice R. but Mr. B. does not believe that will happen to any others. Diary, now I shall pray and pray that Mr. B. will see that it does not.

Papa told me that he wanted me to understand

about the rebellion. He said that he had joined the rebels because he felt so strongly that the injustice in Upper Canada was grievous and had to be stopped. He had finally come to believe that, without rebellion, it never would be stopped. He said that he had no idea what would happen now, but he had learned that, because of the rebellions in both Upper and Lower Canada, the government in England wishes to make life better here. They are sending a man called Lord Durham to be the governor general of both Canadas and to report on "our situation."

He told me that, when he was being marched to the gaol after the battle at Mr. Montgomery's farm, he saw Charlie and Charlie saw him. He does not believe that C. has forgiven him as he has not once visited or sent word. He hoped C. was helping Mr. D. to look after us. (I could not bring myself to tell him that C. has disappeared.) Then he asked if I thought I could ever forgive him. I said that I did forgive him and we both cried again. Then my papa told me that he loved me very much and he said exactly these words, "For myself, I do not regret what I have done, but I shall never forgive myself for causing you and your mother and your brother to suffer so."

He asked if I had read any of the letters he had written to Mama. I had to tell the truth about the note she tore up and I said that I had not seen any others. That was not really a lie and I am sure she has torn those up, too. Papa looked very sad. He said he would write to me in care of Mr. Dewhurst and I said that I would answer all his letters — and that I would come again to visit him.

I asked Papa why he had not been set free when some others had been. He said that he suspected that it had something to do with him being a cousin of Peter Matthews, and also that he and Mr. Hagerman, who is the chief "prosecutor" at the trials, had never been the best of friends.

Truly, Diary, I am not the littlest bit angry with Papa now. How could I have thought I hated him? I love him so much and I have forgiven him entirely. (It is Mama I cannot forgive.) Papa told me I was to be brave. Then it was time for me to leave him. I hated leaving him even though the gaol is so unspeakably dreadful.

Now I know that I should never have thought an unkind thought about kind, kind Mr. Everett C. Dewhurst. It is true that he is stuffy and harrumphy, but I know now that he has been visiting Papa every week since Papa has been in the gaol. He has taken him food, and books to read. As well, he kept not only Papa's Bible, but a few of his law books out from the sale. What a prodigiously good man he is!

I am going upstairs to bed now (did you guess that I was in the kitchen?) and I believe I shall sleep better because I have seen Papa.

Thursday night, 12 April

Mr. Samuel Lount and Cousin Matthews were hanged today in front of the gaol.

Thursday night, 26 April

Dear Diary,

How patient you are! I have not written a word to you in two weeks. I have been so downhearted. I could not write about the hanging. A great many people went to watch. How could they? And it was the day before Good Friday.

It is mournful to have known someone who was hanged. I cannot understand how God can let that happen. Mrs. P. says it is not ours to question but, Diary, I cannot help but question.

Jesse Harvard went to watch the hanging. When he came home, he came into the scullery. His face was a sort of grey-green colour — like mold. For the longest time he did not say a word, he just leaned against the sink looking at me. Then he said he was sorry he had said that about Papa being hanged.

"That will not happen, Arabella," he said. He looked at me as though he cared how I felt and he said it again, "That will not happen."

I was so surprised that not a single word came to my mind to say. I could only nod. He stood for another long time, then he went away. I cannot figure out Jesse Harvard but, Diary, he does not come to torment me anymore and I am glad about that. Also I think better of him for saying what he said.

Sunday, 29 April

Dear Diary,

Dr. S. preached about justice and punishment in church today. I hated it. I wished to talk to Mrs. P. this afternoon, then Cook set me to folding linen and that was that.

Wednesday night, 2 May

Dear Diary,

This afternoon we wrote a letter to Mrs. P.'s cousin in Philadelphia, we read the newspaper (there was nothing in it about the trials), then we began a novel by Miss Jane Austen called *Mansfield Park*. It is a story about society life in England.

Then we did nothing but watch Hector and Dolly. Hector is NOT happy about Dolly living in Mrs. P.'s baby cradle. He yips and yaps at her, then, the instant she puts out a paw, he scurries back into his corner. He squeezes himself down into his bed the way a turtle pulls into its shell, and he whines and whines and whines.

I feel sorry for him — and he has such sad brown eyes. Mrs. P. says he feels usurped (it means to take over someone else's place without their leave) and I can see that he is VERY jealous of Dolly. He should not mind her so much because Dolly prefers me to Mrs. P. She makes that absolutely clear every time I come through the door. Today she leapt into my arms before I even sat down.

I know it is immodest of me but I love knowing that she cares the most for me. Mrs. P. has Hector. She likes Dolly but she likes Hector better.

Friday night, 4 May

Dear Diary,

I did something truly dreadful today. I lost my temper. I lost it completely, totally, absolutely. This is what happened.

Yesterday afternoon, Sukey told me that Cook wished me to make the lettuce beds ready for the new seed. This is one chore I like. Papa and I used to work getting the vegetable beds ready in spring with Jamie, the man who helped us with our gardens. I spent over an hour yesterday pulling out last summer's dead roots and turning over the soil. When I came inside, Cook was furious. She had not sent me out to the garden and she had been looking for me to get the tea ready in the servants' hall. Need I tell you that I did not get my tea. I suspect I should consider myself fortunate that I got my supper.

This morning Sukey stole my one good linen handkerchief. I saw it tucked into the sleeve of her dress. She swore it belonged to her and that the *A* embroidered on it was for her mother whose name was Aggie. Of course I had no way of proving that it was mine but I knew because I was the one who had to spend all those hours embroidering it.

Diary, the rage rose up inside me like a shooting flame. Sukey has tormented and tormented me ever since I came here. When I saw my handkerchief poking out of her sleeve, I exploded like a gun going off.

I shouted and screamed. I grabbed Sukey by her shoulders and shook her. I called her a thief and a liar and an ignorant pig and oh, I cannot remember what else. I was like one possessed of a demon. I was worse than Mama in one of her fits.

Sukey screamed back at me. She called me stuck-up, swelled-headed, snobby and a lot of words I do not know.

She pulled back to strike me when Cook grabbed us both, knocked our heads together and threw us up the back stairs. By the time we got up all those stairs, I was dizzy and my head was hurting too much for me to be really angry anymore. I think I was crying.

Sukey was sobbing great loud sobs and she was still calling me names. When she got to our bedroom door, she turned around and spat at me. "Now you got me into a mess of trouble, you — you get out of here. You get right out of here and take your fancy rag with you. And take your precious writing book, too."

She shoved the handkerchief in my face, she ran into the room, pulled you out from under my spare shift in the dresser and threw you at me. She was still crying and shouting. "I been working in this house three years and more and here you comes dancing in with your uppy ways and, first off, you gets a fancy job with that old woman upstairs. I'm a good worker. I ain't got no pa in the gaol. It ain't right and it ain't fair." I was scared. I picked up the handkerchief and wiped Sukey's spit off my face. I picked you up. I clutched you so hard I wonder you did not break in half. I did not know what to say or what to do. I was sure Sukey would strike me. Instead of that, she cried louder and threw herself down on the bed.

"Did you want to read to Mrs. Parliament?" I could not think of another thing to say.

She sprang up from the bed and shrieked at me, "Read? Where do you think the likes of me would learn to read, you turnip head?" Down she went again.

I sat down on the top step. I was shaking. My head hurt. I felt sick to my stomach. I was beginning to feel a bit ashamed for shouting and screeching and I did not know what to do next.

I did not have to fret about that for long. Cook had us back at work in short order.

Saturday night, 5 May

Dear Diary,

Cook sent Joe upstairs to bring us back to the kitchen yesterday morning. We got a dreadful scold and Cook told us we would both be dismissed if we ever caused such a rumpus in her kitchen again.

She set us to scrubbing floors together. We did not speak to each other all day and we went to bed still not speaking. All the same, I ~~had~~ have a feeling that we have a kind of truce. (I wonder if we might mount a flag of truce over the bed.)

Sunday night, 6 May

Dear Diary,

It was my Sunday afternoon free. I set out for a walk but, just as I started out from the kitchen gate, I saw Betty Marvell and Melissa Partridge coming towards me. I fled back into the house and kept to my room all afternoon. I am such a coward!

I still have a headache.

Dear Diary,

I am sitting in Cook's rocking chair thinking about the fight I had with Sukey and that she said that she could not read. At first, all I could think was, "Good! She did not read my diary!" Now I feel a bit ashamed. I do not believe I have ever thought about knowing how to read or write or do anything else I know how to do. Do you remember when I was unhappy because Sophie would not know where to send me letters? Do you think Sophie knows how to write?

I have not told you this before now, but I really hate it that I cannot go on in school. What I would REALLY like is to go to the college. Of course, girls cannot do that, but I do not care to be an ignorant person. At least I can read and write. I know poor children do not attend Miss St. Clair's school or other schools like it, but are there not schools for poor people like Sukey — or me?

Diary, the world really is NOT fair!

Tuesday, 8 May

Dear Diary,

I have been thinking again about Sukey and that she cannot read or write. I do not like her one bit but I do not like unfairness, either.

Thursday, 10 May

Dear Diary,

I spent almost all yesterday and all today plucking up the courage to ask Sukey if she would like me to teach her to read. I talked to Mrs. P. about it yesterday afternoon and she is "all in favour of the idea."

I finally asked, while Sukey and I were clearing the servants'-hall table of the supper dishes. She was so surprised I thought she was going to drop a whole tray full of dishes. Then she looked at me as though I had called her a dirty name.

She said, "No thank you, Miss high-and-mighty," and she turned from me with her nose in the air.

Diary, I do not understand.

Friday, 11 May

Dear Diary,

Sukey is not speaking to me at all. I do not know whether this is better or worse than when she does speak.

Saturday, 12 May

Dear Diary,

Now I know that Jesse was right. Papa will not be hanged. He is to be sent to Van Dieman's Land along with almost one hundred other rebels. Diary, I am going to put a whole shilling in the collection plate in church tomorrow in thanks.

Wednesday, 16 May, late afternoon

Dear Diary,

Today was my May Wednesday half-holiday and I went to visit Papa without Mr. D. I put on my red and black tartan school dress (Diary, I am truly glad I rescued my clothes from Mama's lodging) and off I went. (I knew I would have to burn this dress, too, but I just did not care.)

I did not really wish to go. Well, part of me did not. It was worse than the time I could not make up my mind to visit Papa the first time. Much worse. I felt like two entirely separate people. One me started out for the gaol quite smartly. The other me turned around and came right back into the house and went up to the top of the attic stairs. The first me turned and went back down the stairs. The second me started to turn back. There we stuck, me one and me two. I felt like Lot's wife who turned into the pillar of salt. I thought I was sure to be stuck there until Cook came and found me. That thought sent me forth again.

Second me's voice kept saying, "Go back home, go back home," all the way, but first me would not turn back. On I marched. (I really did march, left, right, left, right, like the soldiers.) I marched right up to the guard at the front entrance to the gaol and told him I was there to see a prisoner — just as Mr. D. had done.

Diary, it was not so very difficult. The guard opened the door and let me in. Another guard took me to the gaol cell where Papa was, but he would not open the cell door. So I had to talk to Papa through those horrible bars. I could take his hands but we could not hug each other. I told Papa I thought it was because Mr. D. was not with me. He said that I was likely right.

Papa talked about going to Van Dieman's Land. He thinks it will happen next month. He promised he would find a way to write to me from VDL. Then he asked about Mama and Charlie. Diary, I could not look straight into my papa's face and lie about everything. I told him that Charlie had disappeared. I told him that Mama was well and that she had written her relatives in England to ask for passage money for us to go to them. I could not, I just could NOT tell him that I was working in the scullery in Mr. Harvard's house.

I expect he could see that I was distressed because he said that he thought it was best that Mama and I go to England. I kissed him goodbye through those bars.

Good night, Diary.

Thursday, 17 May

Dear Diary,

I came down into the kitchen to write to you last night but I did something that I have promised and promised myself I would not. I cried. I picked up my pencil to write. Then I read what I had written about visiting Papa. I thought about Mama, I thought about Charlie, and I began to cry. I could not stop myself. I cried and I cried in horrible huge sobs. I was so afraid someone would hear me that I went down onto the cellar steps and closed the door. I sat on the dark cellar stairs crying and crying and crying until there cannot have been a single tear left anywhere in me.

It was dreadful, truly, truly dreadful, but now I know that Sophie was right. She told me, after Gran and Granddad died, that a good cry was better than a physic. She was right. She really was right.

Sunday, 20 May

Dear Diary,

I planned to visit Mrs. P., even though it was my Sunday afternoon free, but she was going out driving with Mr. and Mrs. H. I wanted to tell her that Papa was to be sent away to VDL.

I went out walking, instead. The day was so warm

and fine that I did not need my cloak. I spent almost this entire afternoon sitting on a fallen log by a clump of alders where a little stream bubbles into the lake. The red-winged blackbirds were nesting in last year's bulrushes, the marsh was full of bright yellow cowslips and there were clumps and clumps of violets up where I was sitting.

I watched two barges, a bateau and a schooner unloading cargoes at the government wharf. Four men were having a terrible time getting their enormous raft tied up. I could hear their voices and I expect I had better be glad I could not pick out their words. One man became so angry when the raft started floating away after the fifth try that he jumped right into the water and pulled it in. I think he must be very cold!

I sat for such a long time and I was so still that the ducks and the marsh hens ceased their scolding and went about their business as though I were not there. Then, late in the afternoon, a steamship came in and the cannon went off. How those birds did fly off! So did I, for I was sure I was going to be late home. I feel better for having been out with those birds and flowers.

Wednesday, 23 May

Dear Diary,

Tomorrow is Queen Victoria's birthday. I wonder what it feels like to have the whole world celebrate one's birthday?

Thursday, 24 May

Dear Diary,

We had baked chicken for dinner and beautiful cream pudding for afterwards. The banquet at Buckingham Palace cannot have been more splendiferous!

Saturday, 26 May

Dear Diary,

The world is full of surprises! Sukey came into the scullery after dinner today to say that she would like me to teach her to read and write. She said it as though she were bestowing a great favour upon me. I do not really wish to teach her, but I had (in a sort of a way) promised myself I would do it.

Sunday, 27 May

Dear Diary,

I spent the afternoon with Mrs. P. to make up for my free Wednesday afternoon. I told her about Sukey, and she said I might have her old newspapers with which to teach. We talked about Papa. We talked about the Queen's birthday. Mrs. P. thinks the Queen is "enchanting."

We are almost halfway through *Mansfield Park*. I wish Fanny Price, the heroine of this story, were not such a timid mouse. I like stories about girls who are bold and brave.

Monday, 28 May

Dear Diary,

Sukey came to me right after the dinner pots were scrubbed and put away. She had last week's newspaper from Mr. Banks and she wanted a lesson.

It was not diverting! Sukey does not like that I know how to do something she does not, but she very much wishes to know how to read so she will allow me to teach her. Also I have never taught anyone to do anything. I once tried to teach Dolly to close my bedroom door but she would not learn. I think that I may not be able to teach Sukey, either. We spent an entire hour at this task and all that came of it were a lot of very cross words and that Sukey can read the letter *S* in Mr. B.'s newspaper.

I think teaching Sukey to read is going to be a perfectly horrible chore.

Wednesday, 30 May

Dear Diary,

I told Mrs. P. about how horrid the first reading lesson was. Mrs. P. said it is my "worthy cause" and that I must be patient. Diary, I am not sure I CAN be patient with Sukey.

Friday, 1 June

Dear Diary,

Mrs. Harvard came to me in the kitchen this afternoon to give me my half-year pay, two pounds! TWO POUNDS! (I have been working in the scullery for less than five months, she said, so I did not get the full two and a half pounds.) I feel as rich as Midas. I shall buy Papa the notepaper and pencils (pencils will be better than pens and ink) and perhaps some cheese and whatever else Mr. D. considers suitable.

Mrs. H. was very friendly. She told me that she appreciated the time I was spending with Mrs. P. She cannot know how much I love Wednesday afternoons.

Saturday, 2 June

Dear Diary,

There were not so many dishes or pots to clean today. (Both Jesse and Elizabeth have gone to a party at Rosedale House. Also there was stewed rabbit: just one cooking pot.) I had a bit of time to myself so I collected my riches and went off to Mr. Lesslie's shop to buy the stationery and the pencils for Papa. I bought two new ones for myself, too. (I longed to buy myself just one book but I have decided that, if I do not save what I can, I will be stuck in the scullery forever.) Then I went to the Emporium in King Street and bought Papa tea and cheese, a wool muffler, a pair of warm gloves and two cigars. I was so excited about my purchases that I almost left them on the counter.

I had to hurry home or face Cook's wrath but I am QUITE pleased with myself.

Sunday, 3 June

Dear Diary,

In church today, I prayed very hard that Papa might not be sent to VDL. This was my free Sunday afternoon. You will laugh at me because I did not go out. Instead, I went to see Mrs. P. I wished to show her my purchases before I take them to Mr. D. for his approval. She said that I had chosen well. Then, oh, wonderful Mrs. P.! She added another dozen sheets of paper to my stack.

Sukey was cross because she wanted a reading lesson.

Wednesday, 6 June

Dear Diary,

Sukey and I had another reading lesson before tea yesterday. She had kept the newspaper Mr. B. gave her (she said she did not need me to bring them from Mrs. P.) and she has gone out and bought a pencil and several sheets of paper on which she wrote three lines of the letter *S.* I can see how much she wishes to learn and I am trying to be patient but, Diary, Sukey is so SNIPPY. She has no patience. It is as if I were the one trying to learn and she the teacher. Today she learned to read and write her name, both Sukey and Susan. (Sukey is a nickname for Susan. I did not know that and cannot think of Sukey as Susan.)

Today Mrs. P. and I read on in Miss Austen's book. I do wish Fanny Price had more spirit.

Dear Diary,

I sneaked out this afternoon to take Mr. D. my purchases and to ask if he would take me to give them to Papa. I was not sure that I could work up the courage to go there again by myself. What is more, I do NOT want to talk to Papa through those hateful bars. Also, I wished to ask Mr. D. why Papa has not been pardoned while some others are.

Mr. D. told me that I could not see Papa again because the prisoners are to be taken to Fort Henry in Kingston tomorrow. (Tomorrow!) No more than Papa, could he tell me why Papa was not given his freedom. But I have come to believe it really is because Mr. Hagerman does not like Papa. Mrs. P. says that Mr. H. believes that going against the government is as bad as going against God and that he is a "stickler for propriety." She says he really hates WLM and she thinks he likely cannot bear the thought of a barrister like Papa joining with him. I told her that Papa did not like Mr. H. and she said that a great many people do not like Mr. H.

Mr. D. promised to take the things I bought to Papa this evening and he gave me pen and paper to write Papa a note. All I could think to say in my note was that I loved him and I hoped he liked the cheese and I would write to him at Fort Henry. (Fort Henry is a military fort and the rebels are being sent there because they are prisoners of war. Mrs. P.'s newspaper calls them state prisoners.)

Afterwards I felt dreadful that I had not written more but I could not think of another word to say. I shall pray and pray that Papa will not have to go to that terrible island.

Friday night, 8 June

Dear Diary,

The soldiers took Papa and twenty-six other rebels from the gaol today to go to Kingston. They left this afternoon from the Yonge Street wharf. I could not stay away. I sneaked (again) from the house and ran straight to the wharf.

I almost wish I had not gone, it was so horrible. A great many people came to stare and shout horrid things — I daresay they were at the hanging of Mr. Lount and Cousin Matthews. But many were the families of the prisoners. It was easy to see which ones they were because they were like me, trying to reach the men, to take their hands once before — oh the prisoners — oh, Diary, the poor prisoners! my poor, poor Papa!

They looked so sad. They were brave, I know they were, but they looked so sad! They were bound together in heavy iron chains and those hateful soldiers were making them walk too fast up into the steamship. No matter how I pushed my way through the crowd, I could not reach Papa. I waved to him and I called and called. I think he might have heard me because he did look back once. He looked very brave. I shall confess to you, Diary, that I could scarcely see after that because I could not keep from crying. I tried hard not to, but I could not stop myself. Someone put his arm around me and there was Mr. D. He came down to the wharf so that Papa would know there was someone who cared about him. I know he did. I hope, I hope, I hope that Papa knew Mr. D. was there and that I was there. No one should have to go off to the entire other side of the world without knowing that. I am so glad that I bought Papa the stationery so he can write to me. If he wishes to. If they allow him to.

Friday, 15 June

Dear Diary,

Before I write another word, I must tell you the wonderfullest thing in the world. CHARLIE IS ALIVE!! He has written to Jesse and I have the letter. (J. gave it to me.) I will tell you all about it, but first I must, MUST tell you about all the things I have been doing.

I am sure you will have noticed that precisely a

week has gone by since I last wrote. I am sorry. You are still my best friend in all the world but I have been very busy — and NOT just in the scullery.

Last week, the very same day I stole out to bid Papa farewell, Cook came to me when I was scrubbing the potatoes for supper (a whole bucket full and they were old and full of sprouts). I thought she was going to give me what Sukey calls "a lick with the rough side of her tongue," but she was not. She said not a word about my absence from the house. She stood beside me for quite some time while I scrubbed and scrubbed — I did not dare to look at her. Finally she said, "Betty, you writes letters for Mrs. Parliament."

I was sure she was going to tell me that I was not to do it anymore. Then she said, crossly, "Well does yez?" (This is how Cook talks.)

I said, "Yes, I do."

"Well, I wants yez to write one for me," she said.

Diary, I almost splashed potato water in Cook's face because I dropped the potato I was peeling right back into the bucket, I was so surprised (and it was a huge one). I never in the world could have imagined Cook asking me to do anything like that!

So that evening, after I had washed the last supper pot, Cook put a sheet of paper and a pen and an ink bottle on the kitchen table. She sat in her chair by the stove, rocking back and forth. (She does not know that I sit in that chair every night.) She wanted to send a letter to her mother in England. (I wonder if her mother can read. I suppose, if she cannot, she can get someone to read it to her.)

I wrote everything she asked me to but I think she did not really trust me because she kept asking, "Have you put that down? Let me see what that looks like," and other things like that. I think that Cook did not really want to ask me to write that letter. The man who did write letters for her had been a friend of her husband (who died three years ago). He was in the rebellion and has gone to Kingston. (Cook gave me such a look when she said that!) She did not ask me to write about the rebellion, she only wanted me to write that she was safe and well and that the rebellion had left "no lasting harm." (She did tell me to say that a new person was writing the letter but she did not tell me to write that the person was the scullery girl.)

Then I was to write, "your loving daughter, Matilda Eileen Simpson Muldoon." Imagine Cook having first names! Pretty ones like Matilda Eileen. (This is stranger than Sukey's name being Susan.) Now I shall always know that. Matilda Eileen. Cook is Matilda Eileen!

Diary, I shall write the rest tomorrow because I am falling asleep — I wish I were bold enough to make a pot of coffee for myself.

Continued from last night, dear Diary,

That same night, after Cook's letter was finished I went out to walk. I was thinking about Papa — and about writing Cook's letter. I walked along Lot Street towards the sunset. I walked past all the great houses and the Government Common, almost as far as the creek. Suddenly I realized how far I had gone and how dark it was getting and I almost ran home.

When I reached the back entrance of the house, it was locked. I hurried back around to the big front door. I was wondering whether or not I dared knock (and anger Mr. Banks), when I saw a man coming along the street. When he saw me, he started running towards me. I was frightened. I hurried back around towards the kitchen door but he caught up to me. It was Jesse Harvard. Even though I do not like Jesse, I was very glad to see him and not some strange man.

He pushed open the gate to the garden and followed me inside. He sat down on the wooden bench that surrounds the apple tree in the middle of the garden. He asked me to sit there, too — so politely that I did.

For the longest time, he did not say anything. He just kept jiggling his foot. I felt very uncomfortable. Finally he said, "I have been really beastly to you."

What could I say to that, Diary? It is the truth.

He stood up and walked around the bench — twice. All I could see of him was a sort of black shadow because there was no moon that night. Then he sat down. Then he got up. Then he sat down. I slapped mosquitoes away from me. Finally J. said, "I am sorry for being so beastly, Arabella, and I have done something else I am sorry about. I had a letter from Charlie last week and I did not tell you about it."

A letter from Charlie? Diary, I could scarcely take it in. Charlie was alive. Jesse went on talking but I heard not a word until he leaned over and looked right into my face.

He said, "I have not got it here. I shall bring it to you in the morning but I can tell you that he has found work with the Hudson's Bay Company at a place called Trout Lake."

I did not sleep all night for being so glad. The next day and in the days since then, I have been so very happy that Charlie is well and, at the same time, angry with him for leaving without a single thought for Mama and me. In his letter (Jesse brought it to me the next day — in fact, he has let me keep it), he told Jesse that he had written Mama but not had a reply. He asked about Mama and me but not about Papa. He said he was sorry for running off like that. I do not think he will remain sorry for long. Charlie is three years older than I, Diary, but sometimes I feel at least one hundred years older than he.

That was the end of that unbelievable day. Jesse let me into the house by the front door. It was the first time I had been in the family part of the Harvards' house, except for morning prayer time — oh, and Mrs. P.'s apartment.

I am falling asleep, good night.

Sunday, 17 June

Dear Diary,

Is not June the beautifullest month! It was my Sunday afternoon off and I went out to walk. I vowed I would not care if I saw every girl from my class in school and every last one turned away from me.

I walked up College Avenue and through the park and back down Yonge Street. I met not a single, solitary soul I know. I was almost sorry because I had got myself all prepared.

When I came back, Sukey was waiting for me with her newspaper. We sat out in the kitchen garden and, world of surprises, we got on quite well. Sukey was not snippy and she learned a whole sentence. It was in an advertisement for Mr. Morphy's carriages. After she read that, and wrote it on her paper, Sukey started to laugh. She said, "Now I can read that word, d'you think I can get me one of them carriages?"

Do you not think the world is amazing, Diary?

Saturday night, 23 June

Dear Diary,

I do not know whether I am happy or sad. I have had a letter from Papa. He said that he did see me at the Yonge Street wharf when he was led away to Kingston and was glad I was there. He said that Fort Henry is no worse than the gaol in Toronto and that the food is a very little bit better but that he would not serve it to Lord Durham. He said that Lord D. is a reformer and we must all pray that he will bring better government to us. One of the other men in the prison is Mr. Montgomery, who is not to be hanged, after all. He, too, must go to VDL.

Papa told me he loved me and that I must be brave. Diary, I wept all over the letter. I wish I had a likeness of Papa.

Wednesday night, 27 June

Dear Diary,

Mrs. P. and I sat outside this afternoon in a small enclosed garden behind the kitchen garden. We go there now on fine Wednesday afternoons. It is quite, quite wonderful. The pink roses that climb over the wall into the kitchen garden grow here and there are other roses and dahlias and lobelias and marigolds and the tall blue flowers I cannot remember the name of, and they are all in bloom. Butterflies and bees are all over the flowers and the bees' humming is so cheerful, it makes me want to hum, too.

You can imagine how Hector loves being outside. (Of course Mrs. P. brings Hector — and Dolly.) Hector cannot escape the garden but Dolly leaps over the fence to explore the wide, wide world and I always fear she will not come home. She always does.

I have written to Papa. I told him about Charlie's letter. I still have not told him about working in the scullery. I have tried to write cheerful things — Mrs. P. says that is best and I am sure she is right. A man in prison cannot wish to read sad words. So I have been describing what I see when I go out walking. When Joe is busy, Cook sends me to the market and, two days ago, I went to the fish market for a salmon. I do not like the fish market or the smell of fish and I did not like carrying home a bundle of salmon, but I wrote about the fish market (but not about Joe), I wrote about the good weather and I wrote about singing in church (which I still like even though I sit on the benches).

Thursday night, 28 June

Dear Diary,

The Queen is crowned in London, England, "this very day" (Alice Foster said that). I remember that

Mrs. P.'s newspaper had a long description of her coronation robe last year when the dressmakers began sewing it. I thought it very beautiful but I wondered how a person could walk down the long aisle of a big church in such a heavy gown with such a long train on it and not trip all over it.

We were allowed out to see the parades on King Street and the candles lit in all the windows. We had a special dinner to celebrate. We had roasted beef with roasted potatoes and Yorkshire pudding and young greens, and Cook made us both rhubarb tart and a syllabub for afterwards. As well as the beer, there was wine, and there was lemonade for us younger ones. It was like Christmas at midsummer.

Monday, 2 July

Dear Diary,

I spent more than an hour yesterday afternoon with Sukey. She is learning almost faster than I can teach. She wanted to write *Queen Victoria* and *coronation* and then read and write those words over and over and make me look at them.

The rest of the afternoon and last night, I wrote a letter to Charlie. I did not write only cheerful things to him. I wished him to know precisely how truly horrible everything is. I told him about the rooms where Mama is and that she cast me out. I told him where I am and about the dreadful work and how terrible Sukey and Joe and Cook are — and how unkind his friend Jesse was. I recounted every last, dreadful incident I could bring to mind. I really liked writing that letter. Then I felt terrible and tore it all up and wrote another.

In the second letter I told him what has happened to Papa, where Mama is living and where I am and what I am doing. I did not say anything about Cook or Sukey or Joe — or Jesse except that Jesse had given me his letter. I told him about Wednesday afternoons because that is cheerful.

Wednesday, 11 July

Dear Diary,

I cannot keep from thinking about Papa. I dreamed last night that I was trying and trying to reach for his hand, but that he kept being pulled away from me by someone I could not see. I woke up crying. That woke Sukey and she said, "Baby," in a hateful voice and gave me a shove. Oh, Diary, I am so afraid for Papa.

Friday, 13 July

Dear Diary,

Thirty-two more "state prisoners" were sent to Kingston in chains this afternoon. I am sure that this means they will all soon be sent to Van Dieman's Land.

Monday, 16 July

Dear Diary,

I came down to the kitchen last night and the night before. I meant to write but I did not write. I was too distressed. I could not — I cannot — keep from thinking Papa will soon be sent to that terrible island.

I went out yesterday afternoon and sat by the lake and thought about the wide, wide sea. I have not told you this. I know I should never have done so, but, Diary, I had made myself believe that Papa would NOT be sent to that island. I began making daydreams on the day he went off on the steamship to Kingston. In my dreams, he was set free and came back to Toronto to his law office with Mr. D. He found a pretty little house for the two of us (I did not want to imagine Mama in our house and Charlie is now so far away) and a new school for me where I met kindhearted girls who were eager to be my friends (I even gave some of them names. One was Louisa which is Mrs. P.'s name). I imagined that Sophie came back to us to teach me how to cook — you see, I am not quite the proud servant owner I once was — and we were all merry together. Now, ever since I heard about those thirty-two prisoners being sent to Kingston, I have been in the darkest of despairs, just as I was before I met Mrs. P. I can see that Papa and I will never have that happy life. I can see that I am always going to be a scullery maid named Betty in Elizabeth and Jesse Harvard's house with my only pleasure being Wednesday afternoons with Mrs. P.

Yes, I do know what a foolish girl I was but, oh, Diary, I so wanted the dream to come true.

Wednesday, 18 July

Dear Diary,

Lord Durham came to Toronto this afternoon by steamship from Niagara. After what Papa said about him coming to make things better, I had to watch him arrive. It was my free Wednesday so I could do so.

Lord D. is a very great man, an earl (which is a very high English nobleman). Mr. Banks does not entirely approve of him, even though he is an earl, because Lord D. would like to free the rest of the state prisoners. (Oh, Diary, if only he will do this!)

The steamship reached the wharf at four o'clock. The military band was there. The soldiers in their red coats were lined up on either side of the walkway. All the important people were there as well as hundreds of us unimportant ones.

It was a very long while before Lord and Lady Durham came off the boat. When they finally did come, there was an eighteen-gun salute, the band played, and everyone cheered and cheered. Diary, it was very inspiring. Lord Durham is a pale, thin man — but more important-looking than Sir Francis, and much handsomer than Sir George. Lady Durham is very elegant.

Sunday, 22 July

Dear Diary,

I was with Mrs. P. this afternoon because my free Wednesday was last week. I think she is the best person in the world to allow me the free Wednesday. We talked about Lord Durham. I said that I hoped he would do all the things Papa wished him to do. Mrs. P. said she was sure he would do, but she could not say that she was sure he would free all the prisoners.

We read last Thursday's newspaper and two chapters of *Mansfield Park.*

Friday, 27 July

Dear Diary,

Sukey wants to have reading and writing lessons ALL THE TIME. If I am scrubbing pots and she has a moment to spare, there she comes with her newspaper. If I step outside to pick peas, there she is again. Well, I did promise.

Sunday, 29 July

Dear Diary,

I ran away this afternoon right after the dinner dishes were washed. I went where Sukey could not find me. I know it was unkind but it was my free Sunday afternoon and the day was so hot and I did NOT want to sit at the kitchen table when I could be out by the lake. I go to that spot I wrote you about in the spring. I listen to the birds and I watch the boats.

I am not as lonely as I was when I first came to this house. Sukey IS nicer to me now and because she is, Joe is nicer, too. And I have Mrs. P. I love Mrs. P. She is a little like Gran was, warm and kind, and sometimes funny. We laugh together. I do love to be with someone I can laugh with.

After supper, before it got dark, Sukey and I sat in the kitchen garden with Mr. B.'s tired old newspaper. I have some others from Mrs. P. but S. still likes this old one best.

It was really a very good day.

Good night, Diary.

Sunday, 5 August

Dear Diary,

I am out in the kitchen garden tonight. I love this garden. I am glad Cook sends me out to rake and weed and pick the vegetables (but I am careful not to let her know that I like it). The peas are perfect now, the tomatoes are ripening, the beans and radishes are still coming on and the cucumber vines are bursting out of their frame.

I stole out here to see if there was enough light to write by and there is. The moon is full and the garden is all silvery and bright as day. There are the roses climbing over the wall from the other garden, and the sage and savoury and thyme and carroway are doing their herby best to outdo the roses. I have been sitting for quite a few minutes on the bench under the apple tree, swooning from the scent of summer.

Monday, 6 August

Dear Diary,

Mr. Montgomery and some other prisoners escaped from the Kingston prison. Hooray for them! Diary, do you think Papa might be with them?

Tuesday, 7 August

Dear Diary,

I am out in the kitchen garden once more. The night is clear and cool and the moon is still bright enough to write by. The crickets are noisy but there are no other sounds. I think the garden of Eden must have been exactly like this (but I hope there are no snakes here).

I have had a note from Mr. D. to say that Mama wishes to see me. I suppose I had better go on Sunday as it will be my free afternoon.

Sunday, 12 August

Dear Diary,

I went to Mama today. At first she scarcely spoke, she was so angry at me for not coming at once (I believe she expected me to appear the instant the note left her hand). I told her that a scullery girl could not do whatever she wished whenever she wished it. That made her even angrier. She actually got up from her chaise. She said, "Arabella, do you seriously believe that I mean to countenance a daughter of mine working as a menial servant? Well, I shall not."

I did not argue with her. Diary, I have come to see, very clearly, that my mother's mind makes of the world what it wishes to find there. Where she does not wish to find unpleasantness, she makes herself believe it is not there. Once I could not understand how she could do this, but ever since I made myself almost believe Papa could never be transported to VDL, I have understood very well. Now I am so afraid that I am like Mama that I pray every night and every morning that I shall never again allow myself to believe in daydreams.

You will never credit what Mama had to tell me! She has had a letter from her cousin Eustace Parley in Shropshire in England and he has sent money for three sailing-ship passages as well as coach fare to his home. Mama is in raptures and has already instructed (that was the word she used) Mr. D. to "make the arrangements."

I had to tell her that Charlie has found work in the far north. At first she would not believe it. Then she began sobbing that she would never again see her beautiful boy, how could this have happened to her, and ended by shrieking (so loudly I suspect she could be heard all the way to Market Square) about how she had nursed him from a baby and how could he be so ungrateful as to desert her like this. Diary, I wished to (to tell the truth, I started to) walk right out of her room but I knew that, the very next moment, she would throw something, then look for someone to berate, and I felt sorry for Maggie (she was hiding in the front room).

That is just what Mama did. She threw her hand

mirror against the wall and its glass shattered into a million sherds. She shouted that I was no better than Charlie, deserting her in her time of need, going off to be with my friends when she was subjected to such misery. Finally she told me that she would be more than happy if I were out there in the wilderness with my worthless brother and father. I truly believe, Diary, that Mama has made herself forget that Papa was imprisoned. She shouted at me to get out of her sight and I did — and I took Maggie with me.

We went down to Palace Street and walked along the shore, but away from the noisy, smelly fish market and the hammering and shouting at the shipyards. We walked almost as far as Gooderham's windmill. We sat on a big, flat rock at the edge of the lake. Maggie is as retiring as Alice Foster but, after a time, she told me that she is ten years old and an orphan. She is, like me, a girl without any training, so she is really frightened about what will happen to her when Mama leaves. She hopes Mama will give her a "recommend" so she can find another place. I told her I hoped so, too. Maggie went back to Mama and I came home.

MONDAY, 13 AUGUST, 1838

Dear Diary,

Do you remember what day this is? This day is my birthday, my thirteenth birthday. And you are right,

I have not had an elegant birthday party or mountain of birthday gifts (or even a single birthday greeting) because, of course, no one here knows it is my birthday. I believe Mama has forgotten she has a daughter. Papa is so far away and so unhappy that I am sure he will not remember. Charlie never remembers anyone's birthday but his own. So who could know? I, only I (and now you). So I gave myself a birthday gift.

After supper this evening, Cook asked me to write another letter for her. I do not know where I found the courage (perhaps because it is my birthday, perhaps because I am going to England), but, when she said, "Betty, I needs yez to pen me a letter," I said, "I shall do that, Mrs. Muldoon, but my name is not Betty, it is Arabella, and I would prefer you to call me by that name."

At first, I feared Cook would strike me. She gasped. Her eyes squeezed up and her face got very red and her hands went into fists. Then — finally — she said, "hmpf." Then she said, "Well, A-r-a-BELL-a, will yez be so obliged as ta pick up that pen?"

I did. I know there will be a great many horrid extra chores but I have my own name back and it feels like a TREMENDOUS triumph — and a perfect birthday gift!

Wednesday, 15 August

Dear Diary,

Today I had another good afternoon with Mrs. P. We finished *Mansfield Park* and I am glad. I did not like Fanny Price.

Thursday, 16 August

Dear Diary,

It is just as I thought, Cook has piled chore upon chore upon chore on me and I am as Sophie used to say, "bone weary."

Good night.

Saturday, 18 August

Dear Diary,

I wish that I were not going to England. All the way home from the rooms in King Street on Sunday, I thought about Mama and about Charlie and Papa and about that journey and I felt sadder and sadder and sadder. England is so far away — and I fear it will be chock-full of people like Mrs. Milroy and Miss St. Clair. And Mama.

Dear Diary,

In case you are wondering, everything is the miserable same in my kingdom by the kitchen. Sukey has been snarling, which has put Joe in a pet, and Cook keeps finding corners of the kitchen for me to scrub that may not ever have been cleaned before now. As for the above-the-breakfast-parlour world of Mrs. P. and Dolly and Hector, it is as agreeable as the other is horrid.

Mrs. P.'s newspaper is full of talk about Responsible Government. Mrs. P. thinks, as Papa does, that without the rebellion, Lord Durham would not be here to make this come about.

It is still perfect in the kitchen at night.

Sunday, 26 August

Dear Diary,

Mr. D. sent me a note today to say that he believes the prisoners at Fort Henry will soon be sailing to Van Dieman's Land. I have been certain, certain, certain EVERY SINGLE DAY since those last prisoners went to Kingston that this would happen. Diary, I am very sad.

It rained all day and it is raining tonight. It was my free Sunday and I went up to visit with Mrs. P. this afternoon (before I had Mr. D.'s note). She says she is always glad to see me. She sent me down to the kitchen for tea. Of course Cook was not pleased. I told Mrs. P. about going to England. She said she was happy for me but that she would miss me dreadfully. I do not wish to make Mrs. P. sad but I did feel a bit glad that she will miss me.

I cannot write out in the garden (your pages would be absolutely ruined). So I am, once again, in Cook's chair in the kitchen. It is so hot that, if the air were any wetter, the kitchen would be full of steam.

I feel as though it is raining inside me and I truly do not wish to go to England with Mama.

Tuesday, 28 August

Dear Diary,

Today I scrubbed thirty-five tired old potatoes, thirty-three carrots and more pots than I care to mention.

Wednesday, 29 August

Dear Diary,

Well, I did not write much last night, did I? I am feeling more the thing tonight.

We had a perfect afternoon in the garden. Mrs. P. asked Cook for tea and lovely lemon tarts and I brought it out to us. (You can imagine how much Matilda Eileen Muldoon liked giving me those tarts!) Then I read to Mrs. P., first from the newspaper and then from a new book by Mrs. Traill entitled *The Backwoods of Canada.* I like it better than *Mansfield Park.*

Thursday, 30 August

Dear Diary,

I have made a very big decision. A VERY big decision. I did not sleep all last night (you can imagine how tired I was when all the cocks in the neighbourhood began to crow and I had to get up!). But I did get all my work done today as well as the extra errands and scrubbing Cook made me do to pay for the tea I had in the garden with Mrs. P. yesterday.

All night I thought about Papa and I worried and worried about going to England with Mama. You know how I hate working in the scullery and how I hate the way Cook and Sukey and Joe are. I hate that you and Mrs. P. are my only friends. But I hate, even more, the thought of going away from Upper Canada. So I have decided NOT TO GO TO ENGLAND WITH MAMA.

Do you think I am mad? I think I might be because I shall not have to work in a scullery in England — but I think that I shall have to work at something. In *Mansfield Park,* Fanny Price is some kind of servant even though she is a relative of the wealthy family and she does not receive any payment for her services. I believe that I would be like that with Mama's relatives. Also, all the people would be strangers who would look down on me because I am a Canadian (the way Miss St. Clair and Mrs. Milroy do).

No, I shall not go.

Sunday, 9 September

Dear Diary,

It was my afternoon off and I went to Mama after dinner. I told her I would not go with her to England. All she said was, "Arabella, who will look after me on the journey?" She did not get up from the chaise longue.

I said, "take Maggie," and I left her. I would not let her see my tears. Oh, Diary, I do not mind Cook's and Sukey's and Joe's insults or the slights from old neighbours and friends or anything else the way I mind that Mama does not care for me. If I ever have a little girl, I shall . . .

Monday, 10 September

Dear Diary,

I could not write any more about Mama last night — nor can I tonight — nor perhaps ever again, but I do need to tell you that I am holding firm about not going to England. I cannot think that Mama's English cousins will want me any more than she does. What is more, Diary, though Charlie is not in Upper Canada, he is on this continent and, as well, when Papa's prison term is complete and he comes home, it might be that we COULD find a pretty little house. I have learned so much that now I think I could look after Papa — and Charlie, too, if he were to come home. Diary, I know I am daydreaming again, but only the very littlest bit.

Thursday, 13 September

Dear Diary,

I cannot believe that I really, honestly, truly told Mama that I would not go to England! I went to see Mr. D. in his office yesterday afternoon because he is "making the arrangements" for the voyage. Mrs. P. said she was happy to give me the hour away. Mrs. P. is so generous — and I believe she is pleased that I am not going away.

Mr. D. was surprised. He told me that I would have the life of a gentlewoman in England and grow up to marry a gentleman. He asked me several times if I was absolutely certain that I wished to continue to work in the scullery at Harvard House. I said, "Yes. I do not wish to go to England."

Mr. D. said, "Arabella, you are a brave girl, a mite headstrong, mind you, but brave." Diary, I was pleased that he said I was brave (I do not feel one bit brave!) but I was SO embarrassed! I said thank you — I think I said thank you — and I stood up to take my leave. Then Mr. D. asked me if I would come for tea on Sunday week (my next free Sunday afternoon). He said, despite the fact that I had refused earlier invitations, he hoped that I would accept, as Anne and Jenny so wished me to come.

Diary, Mr. D. has been so kind and he HAS invited me several times. I could not say no, so I am to go to tea *chez* Dewhurst on Sunday. (You see, I have not forgotten all the French that Madame Rouselle taught us at school.)

Wednesday, 19 September

Dear Diary,

This was my Wednesday afternoon free. I would have spent some of it with Sukey's reading and writing but she told me that she was busy writing a letter and would not need my "assistance." Diary, Sukey is a great trial — but she HAS learned amazingly. I am quite pleased with myself.

Dear Diary,

I had such a good afternoon. It was the best free Sunday afternoon since I came to this house. The day was fine and I set out for the Dewhurst house in Graves Street as soon as I had finished reading to Mrs. P. (I told her I would come directly after tea to read Thursday's newspaper.)

I very nearly did not go. I spent the last three evenings (now you know why I was not writing to you) washing and pressing my one good summer gown (the peach muslin with the blue flowers on it) only to discover that it no longer fits me. Diary, I have come to be at least two inches taller since last summer — and, of course, I have not had occasion to wear that dress until now. So I had no choice but to wear one of the horrid grey raggedy THINGS that I wear every day. I did feel dreadful having to go to tea in it but I had to go, I had promised Mr. D.

I need not have fretted. Anne and Jenny came to the door when I knocked and they did not say a word about my grey rag — or even give it looks — but took me straight through to the garden where tea things were laid out. There we sat eating cakes and drinking tea as though I were an ordinary girl, come for the afternoon — but I am not ordinary any more and it could not be an ordinary afternoon. Jenny began to talk about school, and then she blushed and stopped. Anne began to tell me about a birthday party she had gone to and then she stopped. We could not talk of school or parties or any of the things I used to talk about with my friends.

Then J. began talking about the new baby. His name is George. (That makes seven boys in the D. family, and two girls — what a lot of boys!) J. asked if I wished to see him and, of course, I did. He is beautiful. Do you not think babies are beautiful, Diary? Baby George is three months old. He is the colour of the pale pink roses that grow along Mrs. P.'s garden wall, he has fuzz on his head like the fuzz on a peach and he smiles and smiles and smiles all the time. Diary, I wished I could take him home.

When I thought that, a picture popped into my head of me bringing baby George into the servants' hall at supper and how comical everyone around the table would look. I laughed out loud. Then I had to tell A. and J. what was funny. We laughed and laughed and made up stories about what everyone would say. So then I had to tell them about Cook and Sukey and Joe and Mr. Banks and everyone and, suddenly, I was telling them all about life at Harvard House. A. looked sad but J. — well, I have told you about J. so you cannot be surprised when I tell you that she leapt to her feet and wanted to go straightaway to tell Sukey how dreadful she is. Then she wanted to say to Cook, "Matilda Eileen Muldoon, you are a tyrant," and tell Joe he has a hateful laugh and, oh, any number of bold things. I believe that if WLM had had J. to fight with him, the rebels would have won their fight and Papa would be home and everything would be as it ought to be.

Monday, 24 September

Dear Diary,

I think perhaps I ended my visit with you a bit abruptly last night. I ought not to have allowed myself to think about Papa. I was not thinking about him yesterday when I came back here, I was thinking about Anne and Jenny as I carried my new wardrobe — oh, how could I have forgotten to tell you about that? Mrs. D. had taken in two of A.'s shifts and three of her outgrown gowns for me (A. is still taller and fatter than I) and given me a new pair of drawers, two pairs of mended stockings and a pair of shoes which Jenny has outgrown (even though she is younger than I). So now I have shoes without holes and three (!) muslin dresses that fit me and are not much worn. One is the colour of spring daffodils and has a bit of lace at its neck, one is pale blue with a sash of darker blue, and one is white with tiny flowers embroidered all over it. I like that one the best.

When I came into the kitchen with my new dresses,

Sukey was just coming in from her afternoon. She looked at the dresses in such a way, Diary, that, at once, I felt guilty that I had them. She turned from me quickly and said not a word. I said nothing to her, either, and took my new wardrobe upstairs.

Later (on my tower steps)

Dear Diary,

I could not sleep for thinking about Sukey. Diary, I am really not the unluckiest person in the world. I have Mrs. P. and I have the Dewhurst family who are kind to me. I have known how to read and write for years and I know many other things Sukey does not.

Diary, I may be the selfishest person I know.

Still Later

Dear Diary,

I mean to give Sukey one of my gowns — but not the white one with the flowers on it.

I feel much better.

Tuesday, 25 September

Dear Diary,

I have not given Sukey the gown yet. Do you remember what she said when I asked if she wanted me to teach her to read? I know now that she was insulted. I did not feel insulted when Mrs. D. gave me the clothes, but perhaps that is not the same as me giving things to Sukey. Diary, what shall I do?

Wednesday, 26 September

Dear Diary, dear, dear Diary,

I AM GOING TO LEAVE THE SCULLERY. Can you believe this? Can you truly believe this? Of course you cannot because I can scarcely believe it. Well, it is TRUE!

I went, as usual, to Mrs. P.'s rooms after dinner today. It was raining (it is still raining — quite ferociously, I can hear it at the kitchen window) so we did not go out into the garden. After we had our tea, and Dolly had settled into my lap and allowed me to read the correspondence (one letter from the niece in Picton and one from the cousin in Pennsylvania) and a chapter of Mrs. Traill's book, Mrs. P. said, "Now, Arabella, I have a proposition for you."

She was smiling so I knew it could not be something disagreeable. Then she asked me this amazing question, "Would you be willing to become my companion?"

Diary, at first I did not understand. I thought I already was Mrs. P.'s companion and I said that. Mrs. P. said she meant that she wished me to be her companion, not only on Wednesday afternoons but every day of the week. She explained it carefully. I am to earn a great deal more money than I am earning now. I am to live in one of the upstairs rooms in the family part of the house and eat with the family. (I wonder if I am to sit with the family in church.) When I am not needed, I may do whatever I wish and, more than this — even more than this — she wishes me to continue in school.

Mrs. P. said that her daughter is agreeable to this plan, but that, first, a new scullery maid will have to be found.

For some time after she explained it all to me, I could not think of a word to say. Not one.

Then Mrs. P. said something almost more astonishing. She said, "You must know, Arabella, that you have become very dear to me."

Diary, I knew no such thing. I love Mrs. P. You know that I do, and I have thought that she liked me to come to her, but I never thought — NEVER thought — that she cared for me. I sat in my chair as stiff and silent as the china figure on top of Mrs. P.'s bookshelf but, suddenly, in my heart I was singing.

"Well, Arabella, do you want to do this?" Mrs. P. asked.

I nodded. I said "Yes" quite loudly. Then I could not keep myself from jumping up from my chair and hugging her.

Diary, do you think this is another daydream?

Thursday, 27 September

Dear Diary,

It is not a daydream and it is settled. As soon as a new scullery maid is found, I am to have a room all to myself on the third floor of the family part of the house, next to Alice Foster, near the nursery. I will spend my days with Mrs. P. and in school, but NOT at Miss St. Clair's school.

I can scarcely believe this has happened to me, Arabella Eleanora (not Betty) Stevenson. Wonderful, marvellous, amazing Mrs. P. She has twirled my life about like the colours in the kaleidoscope that Granddad once gave to Charlie.

No more scullery. No more sharing a bed with Sukey. No more rough side of Matilda Eileeen Muldoon's tongue. No more wearing these horrible grey dresses. Everything will be better — but, Diary, one thing about this new turn in my topsy-turvy life distresses me. I really do not wish to eat my meals with the Harvard family. I think I do not mind Mr. and Mrs. H. — or Charlotte, if she eats at the downstairs table — but Elizabeth and Jesse I do mind (possibly not Jesse so very much now). How can I talk or act as I once did with E. — or any of her friends who used to be my classmates? I asked Mrs. P. if it might not be better for me to continue to eat in the servants' hall. She said that she felt it to be important for me to take my "rightful place in society once more."

That is exactly what I promised myself I would do, do you remember? Now I fear that I might be, in the Harvard family, just what I feared I would be in England with Mama. I might be like one of Miss Austen's "poor relations."

I do know that I will like it better than working in the scullery. Also I will still be here in Canada — AND I will be earning better wages and can save towards the purchase of the house Papa and I shall have some day.

Friday, 28 September

Dear Diary,

Everything happens at once. Mr. D. sent me a note last night to tell me that Mama has passage on a steamship leaving tomorrow noon for Kingston (from there she will go by coach to New York and then sail to England). If I would like, he will ask permission from Mrs. H. to take me to bid her farewell. I told the boy who brought the note that I would like him to do that.

I am not at all sure that I would like it but I cannot know that Mama is going away forever without bidding her goodbye.

Dear Diary,

Mama has gone and she has taken Maggie with her. Maggie was very happy to be going. I am very happy not to be going. All the same, I felt truly forlorn when I saw the last of the steamship pass the lighthouse on its way to Kingston.

Mama told me she was pleased for me that Mrs. Harvard has taken me into her family.

Saturday, 6 October

Dear Diary,

A new scullery girl has come. Her name is Dorothea and, I am pleased to report to you, she is taller and bigger than Cook (much too big for dead Betty's dresses) and looks to be as strong as a team of oxen. I cannot think that Matilda Eileen Muldoon will tell her she is to be called Betty.

I am living in a new tower bedroom. It is quite small, but, compared to the attic room with Sukey, it is a princess's *boudoir* and I am *une vraie princesse*. There is a small fireplace in this room. My bed is the spool bed that was Mrs. P.'s when she was a girl and it has a feather mattress and a pillow and a warm quilt. I have a dresser all to myself and the dearest little chintz-covered wing chair by the window, with a table and a lamp beside it (not as beautiful as Mrs. P.'s lamp but very pretty). A bookcase is squeezed against the wall on the other side of my bed and, already, there are books in it, including a Bible and a prayer book.

I have new shoes and three new gowns suitable for school, another for Sundays and another for special occasions. I have a new blue wool cloak and a bonnet to match. Mrs. P. is NOT poor and she insists that, now that I am "securely in her employ," she means to see that I am "properly clothed."

I begin at Miss Hussey's School on Teraulay Street on Monday. It is not as fashionable as Miss St. Clair's School and Mrs. P. thinks I will like it very well. She knows Miss Hussey.

Sunday, 7 October

Dear Diary,

I cannot think how it came about, but I did not see until now that I have come to your very last two pages. I will miss you terribly. I would purchase a new diary so as to continue writing but it would not be you and I do not wish to write on a stranger's pages. So this will be farewell.

Before it is farewell forever, I had best tell you precisely how things are for me now.

Of course Cook told Sukey about me before I

could tell her myself. S. said in her best hateful voice, "I suppose you will be too grand for any of us in the servants' hall, now."

I told her that I was not a bit grand, and that I did not wish to stop being with her or the other servants — or to stop writing Cook's letters. Also I gave her one of Anne Dewhurst's dresses and she did not refuse it. We let it out together.

Mrs. P. means me to become exactly as I was before the rebellion happened and Papa went to the gaol but, Diary, I do not believe that is possible. Once I was Arabella Stevenson who had a mother and father and brother and attended Miss St. Clair's School for Young Ladies and had friends and went to parties and never worked at anything. Then the whole world collapsed and I had a dead girl's name, was a person no one wished to have anything to do with, and who had to work terribly hard. Then I found Mrs. P. and I became Arabella once more. But I am not Arabella the way I once was.

Diary, do you know what my rightful place in society is? I think my rightful place is with Mrs. P. and the Dewhurst family and Papa and Charlie and even Sukey and Cook (though I still do not much like either one of them). I am still a servant, even though I am now an "upper" servant (imagine that!) and I am still the rebel's daughter.

Diary, you have been my very best friend in all the

world — and you know how grievously I have needed a friend. When I have enough money, I am going to buy you a beautiful leather box where you will be very comfortable and I can keep you forever.

Farewell, dear Diary, farewell.

Post Scriptum: my favourite of all your pages is the August 13 page.

What Became of Them All

Arabella finished her formal schooling when she was fourteen. She would have loved to go on to the Grammar School and then on to King's College (later the University of Toronto) but, in those years in Upper Canada, women were not admitted to secondary (then called grammar) schools, colleges or universities. She continued with her studies on her own, with the help of Mr. Dewhurst and anyone she could persuade to instruct her in the subjects in which she was interested, and lived with the Harvard family as Mrs. Parliament's companion until Mrs. Parliament died. (She did eat her meals with the family and Elizabeth did not snub her.)

Mrs. Parliament died in 1848 at the age of eighty, leaving Arabella enough money on which to live comfortably for the rest of her life. Arabella never married and her dream of a pretty little house where she would live with her father never came true.

Her father was pardoned, after two years of hard labour in Van Dieman's Land. He planned to come home, but the hard work and poor food had left him in very ill health and he was afraid to attempt the long voyage. So he stayed in Van Dieman's Land (renamed Tasmania in 1856). For the next five years, for small fees (often none at all), he helped with the legal work for ex-convicts and for poor immigrants wanting to buy land and make new lives for themselves. He became involved in the politics of the island and worked for fair and honest government there. He died in the summer of 1847 and was buried in Hobart, where he had settled. Arabella bought a house for herself on Graves Street (later Simcoe Street) near the Dewhurst family home. She set up a school there for working girls. With the help of friends she had met through Mrs. Parliament and the Harvard family, and many bazaars to raise money, she made sure that tuition and books would be free. She devoted herself to her school, not only running it but teaching, until she was almost eighty. She was a kind but strict teacher and never let a girl leave her school who could not, at the least, read, write and add, subtract and multiply numbers.

Arabella and her father corresponded faithfully during his imprisonment and the seven years he lived after it. His tales and his drawings of cockatoos, kangaroos, "duck-bill moles" and other exotic creatures that lived on that faraway island instructed and intrigued generations of Arabella's students.

Arabella's mother lived to be seventy-five in genteel poverty on her cousin's estate in England. She complained bitterly every day of her life about how badly she had been used. Arabella wrote to her mother dutifully, once a year, but never received a letter in reply.

Charlie worked for the Hudson's Bay Company for seven years, after which he left to homestead in what is now southern Saskatchewan. He married the daughter of a fellow homesteader and they had four sons, all of whom stayed in the west, and one daughter, Eliza, who went to Toronto as a student and stayed to teach in her Aunt Arabella's school. When Arabella retired, Eliza took over the running of the school.

Anne Dewhurst died of diphtheria at the age of eighteen. Jenny married twice. Her first husband was a captain in the 85th regiment stationed at Fort York in Toronto. He was killed bear hunting six months after they were married. Her second husband was a doctor from New York. They had four children, all of whom survived to adulthood, but Jenny died when the last one was born, a girl she named Arabella.

The seven Dewhurst boys all lived to adulthood and went west, every one of them. It therefore fell to Arabella, who remained close to that family all her life, to care for Mr. and Mrs. Dewhurst in their old age. She moved into their house when the last boy moved out. Around that time, Jenny's widowed husband went back to the United States with his oldest three children. He left baby Arabella with her grandparents and her "auntie."

Mrs. Dewhurst died at age seventy-five but Mr. Dewhurst lived to be a vigorous ninety-seven. To the last, he engaged Arabella in many spirited discussions about the law and about politics. He confessed to her, one day when he was quite old, that he had always greatly admired her father and wished that he, too, had had the courage to fight for what he believed to be right.

Jesse Harvard grew up to study law. He surprised everyone by becoming one of the quiet, hard-working movers of Responsible Government in Upper Canada. He never married. He proposed marriage to Arabella Stevenson the day after he took his bar examinations, and five more times after that. She refused him every time but, over the years, they became close friends and remained so until Jesse died at age fifty.

Sukey was determined to do as Arabella had, and become a teacher. Instead, she fell in love with a fisherman, married him and had eleven children, eight of whom lived to grow up. She and Arabella were not always easy or comfortable with each other, but they stayed friends all their lives. Sukey's children were all devoted to "Auntie Belle." Three of the girls attended her school and one went on to teach.

Mr. Banks, Mrs. Evans and Matilda Eileen Muldoon grew old in the service of the Harvard family. Alice Foster spent her working life as the shy, quiet nursemaid to a long series of Toronto children. Joe disappeared from Toronto when he was fifteen years old.

Historical Note

The 1837 rebellions in Upper and Lower Canada came about for many reasons. Most historians regard the foremost reason to be the lack of consideration the upper-class legislators had for the needs of poorer people. Another element was the resentment some immigrants felt over the preferential treatment that British immigrants received.

In Upper Canada (now Ontario) these legislators were called the Family Compact by their detractors, because they were such a tightly knit group of wealthy men. In Lower Canada (now Quebec) the British officials and the wealthy French who supported them were called the Château Clique because the government offices were in the Château St-Louis. In both provinces these men believed in the rule of the wealthy upper class and a British way of life.

In Lower Canada the most prominent Reform leaders were Wolfred Nelson and Louis Joseph Papineau. In Upper Canada, William Lyon Mackenzie and Samuel Lount both sat in the Legislature for the Reform Party, in opposition to the Family Compact conservatives.

Sir Francis Bond Head's conservative Tories in Upper Canada managed to defeat the Reform Party in the election of 1836, after which Sir Francis replaced all Reform-leaning judges with men expressly loyal to him, and made sure that Reformers' bills and petitions did not go forward. The Reformers, angry at being thwarted, did their best to stall Tory bills, with the result that the two sides were at constant loggerheads.

In addition, years of poor harvests had brought severe food shortages and, in some places, extreme hunger, and the Tories and their British governors would do nothing to help. (In fact, the rebellion in Upper Canada has often been called The Farmers' Rebellion.) Mackenzie and like-minded men decided to take dramatic action.

The first battle of the rebellions was in Lower Canada at the village of St. Denis on the Richelieu River on November 23, when the rebels (called *les Patriotes*) under Wolfred Nelson met Colonel Charles Gore and his British troops. *Les Patriotes* won that battle. In a panic Sir Francis Bond Head sent most of the soldiers stationed at Fort York in Toronto to Lower Canada to help put down the rebellion.

Seizing the moment, Mackenzie rallied his rebels and, on December 7, struck at Montgomery's Tavern and at the Don River bridge in Toronto. He failed. There was another unsuccessful skirmish near Brantford, Ontario, a few days later and other equally unsuccessful raids the following year at Short Hills and at Prescott.

In both provinces, most of the leaders escaped into the United States. In Lower Canada, twelve *Patriotes* were hanged and fifty-eight were sent to the penal colonies in Australia and Van Dieman's Land. In Upper Canada, ninety-two were sent to the penal colonies, many more were sent into exile, and many died in prison. In Toronto, only Samuel Lount and Peter Matthews were hanged. Six others in western Upper Canada were hanged in London.

The results of the rebellions meant great hardship for not only the men involved in them but for their families. In many cases, their land and homes were confiscated, leaving them destitute and unwelcome in their neighbourhoods. Churches took some responsibility for helping widows and orphans. However, without the help of family or friends, the destitute were often left to find what work they could in the breweries, bakeries or foundries, to live in the jails or to starve on the streets, as there were neither alms-houses nor poorhouses in Toronto at that time.

A great many people in Upper Canada who were sympathetic to the Rebels — and even more sympathetic to the Reformers — went to live in the United States. They feared that the Family Compact would always have a stranglehold on their province. (One of the families that left was the Edison family, whose descendant was the American inventor Thomas Alva Edison).

The government in London, England, had known for some time that the political situation was turbulent in both Canadas. After the rebellions, John George Lambton, the Earl of Durham, a known supporter of political reform, was sent from England in 1838 to be the Governor General of British North America. He was asked by the Crown to make recommendations for the future governing of the Canadian colonies. Among other reforms, his 1839 Report on the Affairs of British North America led to the union of the two Canadas (to be called Canada East and Canada West) and brought about what was called Responsible Government. Its intention was that the government in power in both legislatures have the agreement of the majority of the legislators in order to carry out its programs. This marked the end of the absolute control of the Family Compact in Upper Canada and of the Château Clique in Lower Canada.

Robert Baldwin, the lawyer who had defended the political prisoners in Toronto in 1838, and Louis-Hippolyte La Fontaine, a moderate Reformer in Lower Canada, were the chief influence on Lord Durham's planning for Responsible Government. However, Responsible Government did nothing to make things better for working-class people in either province. That took a great many years and the tireless efforts of many Reformers in both districts. Labouring people worked long hours, generally for very low wages, often in poor conditions. There were no safety measures until labour unions were well established, many not until the mid-twentieth century or even later. There were no pensions, no health insurance and no welfare. Poor people who got sick often lost their jobs and had to depend on family and friends or what meagre charity their cities or towns meted out, since these had no formal social agencies to help the poor until the 1860s.

In Canada, there were no laws regarding the employment of children before the 1870s. These were few, and ill observed, until the 1920s and 1930s, when strict laws about both child employment and education were enacted and, generally, enforced. As for domestic servants, the passage of time and universal education brought about the possibility of more attractive work elsewhere and, eventually, better working conditions.

Poor children were very lucky if they had any schooling through much of the nineteenth century. Schools before the 1840s were financed by government grants and tuition fees. While wealthy citizens like Jesse Ketchum gave money to establish schools, admission to those schools was not free. Toronto brewer Enoch Turner established the city's first free school, the Enoch Turner School, in 1848. (His schoolhouse is still standing on Trinity Street in Toronto.)

When Methodist minister and educator Egerton Ryerson became Chief Superintendent of Education for Canada West in 1844, one of the first things he did was to work for province-wide free education. But this did not actually happen until the Schools Act of 1871. Only then did Dr. Ryerson and other like-minded men start the push for compulsory elementary education for both girls and boys. By the 1870s, both were being educated in secondary schools. The Home District Grammar School in Toronto (later Jarvis Collegiate Institute), established in 1807, only began admitting girls in 1864. As for colleges and universities, the University of Toronto first admitted women in 1884.

Young women like Arabella Stevenson had to get their education where they could find it.

Skaters on Toronto Harbour in 1835, with Gooderham's Windmill in the background.

Printed "broadsides" or "broadsheets" such as these were posted during elections, urging people either to align with the goals of the reformers, or to support Sir Francis Bond Head.

Rebels march down Yonge Street toward Toronto, some armed with rifles, but many carrying only tools such as staves or pikes.

Prisoners from southwestern Ontario are taken to jail in a cart after the rebellion there failed.

A.D. 1837.

PROCLAMATION.

BY His Excellency SIR FRANCIS BOND HEAD,
Baronet, Lieutenant Governor of Upper Canada, &c. &c.

To the Queen's Faithful Subjects in Upper Canada.

In a time of profound peace, while every one was quietly following his occupations, feeling secure under the protection of our Laws, a band of Rebels, instigated by a few malignant and disloyal men, has had the wickedness and audacity to assemble with Arms, and to attack and Murder the Queen's Subjects on the Highway—to Burn and Destroy their Property—to Rob the Public Mails—and to threaten to Plunder the Banks—and to Fire the City of Toronto.

Brave and Loyal People of Upper Canada, we have been long suffering from the acts and endeavours of concealed Traitors, but this is the first time that Rebellion has dared to shew itself openly in the land, in the absence of invasion by any Foreign Enemy.

Let every man do his duty now, and it will be the last time that we or our children shall see our lives or properties endangered, or the Authority of our Gracious Queen insulted by such treacherous and ungrateful men. MILITIA-MEN OF UPPER CANADA, no Country has ever shewn a finer example of Loyalty and Spirit than YOU have given upon this sudden call of Duty. Young and old of all ranks, are flocking to the Standard of their Country. What has taken place will enable our Queen to know Her Friends from Her Enemies—a public enemy is never so dangerous as a concealed Traitor—and now my friends let us complete well what is begun—let us not return to our rest till Treason and Traitors are revealed to the light of day, and rendered harmless throughout the land.

Be vigilant, patient and active—leave punishment to the Laws—our first object is, to arrest and secure all those who have been guilty of Rebellion, Murder and Robbery.—And to aid us in this, a Reward is hereby offered of

One Thousand Pounds,

to any one who will apprehend, and deliver up to Justice, WILLIAM LYON MACKENZIE; and FIVE HUNDRED POUNDS to any one who will apprehend, and deliver up to Justice, DAVID GIBSON—or SAMUEL LOUNT—or JESSE LLOYD—or SILAS FLETCHER—and the same reward and a free pardon will be given to any of their accomplices who will render this public service, except he or they shall have committed, in his own person, the crime of Murder or Arson.

And all, but the Leaders above-named, who have been seduced to join in this unnatural Rebellion, are hereby called to return to their duty to their Sovereign—to obey the Laws—and to live henceforward as good and faithful Subjects—and they will find the Government of their Queen as indulgent as it is just

GOD SAVE THE QUEEN.

Thursday, 3 o'clock, P. M.
7th Dec. *1837*

☞ The Party of Rebels, under their Chief Leaders, is wholly dispersed, and flying before the Loyal Militia. The only thing that remains to be done, is to find them, and arrest them.

R. STANTON, Printer to the QUEEN'S Most Excellent Majesty.

Sir Francis Bond Head's Proclamation offering £1000 for the capture of W.L. Mackenzie and £500 for David Gibson, Samuel Lount, Jesse Lloyd or Silas Fletcher.

183

Members of the 1st Regiment of Dragoon Guards escort captured rebels to jail.

Toronto's jail at the left, in which many of the prisoners were held following the rebellion. Some died there before they were either pardoned or sent to Van Diemen's Land.

A "Rebellion Box," typical of those carved by prisoners awaiting transport to Van Diemen's Land for taking part in the rebellion.

The hanging of Samuel Lount and Peter Matthews. Their bodies were taken from Potter's Field and moved to the Toronto Necropolis Cemetery in 1859, where a monument was erected to their memory. An historical plaque stands on Toronto's Yonge Street at the site of Montgomery's Tavern.

West Lodge, one of the more stately Toronto homes.

Four-poster beds, one with side curtains — typical of a bedroom in a well-to-do home.

Jesse Ketchum's Tannery was one of Toronto's first industries. Ketchum provided funds to establish schools in the city. The school named after him still exists today.

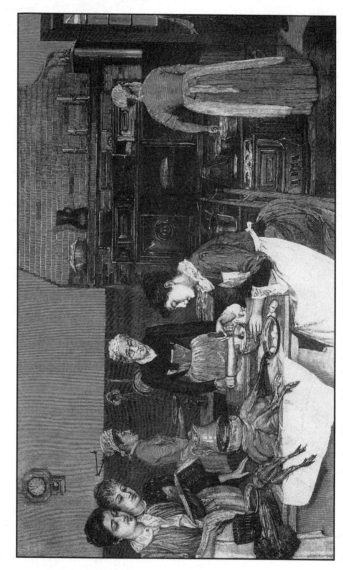

Servants prepare the family's meal in the kitchen of a well-to-do late-nineteenth-century home.

Soup kitchens were available in the colder months to assist the poor and destitute. Most soup kitchens would not have been as large as the one shown in this image.

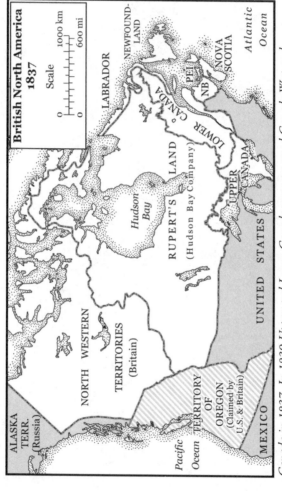

Canada in 1837. In 1839 Upper and Lower Canada were renamed Canada West and Canada East.

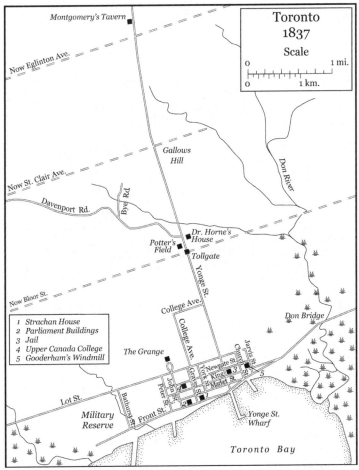

Toronto and area in 1837, showing various landmarks and sites of skirmishes between the Rebels and the government forces. Lot Street is now Queen Street (renamed in 1840 after Queen Victoria), Market Street is Wellington, Newgate Street is Adelaide and Graves Street is Simcoe.

Acknowledgments

Grateful acknowledgment is made for permission to reprint the following:

Cover portrait: Detail from *Portrait of a Young Girl* by William Bouguereau, ArtRenewal 23385.
Cover background: *71st Regiment, Highland Light Infantry: Heavy Marching Order,* Library and Archives Canada C-003653.

Page 179: William Armstrong, detail from *Winter Scene on the Bay,* Toronto Public Library, Acc JRR 842.
Page 180 (upper): *1836. Farmers.* Baldwin Room Broadsides, Toronto Public Library.
Page 180 (centre): *1841. Elections.* Baldwin Room Broadsides, Toronto Public Library.
Page 180 (lower): *1836. Reform Alliance Society.* Baldwin Room Broadsides, Toronto Public Library.
Page 181: C.W. Jefferys, *Rebels Marching Down Yonge Street to Attack Toronto, December, 1837,* Library and Archives Canada C-013988.
Page 182: *71st Regiment, Highland Light Infantry: Heavy Marching Order,* Library and Archives Canada C-003653.
Page 183: *Sir Francis Bond Head's Proclamation offering £1000,* Library and Archives Canada C-012176.
Page 184: Michael Angelo Hayes, *King's Regt. of Dragoon Guards, Winter Costume in Canada,* Library and Archives Canada C-006223.
Page 185 (upper): *Jail (1827–1840), King St. E., ne. cor. Toronto St.,* Toronto Public Library, T 11963.
Page 185 (lower): "Rebellion Box," courtesy of The Blue Pump, photograph by Catherine London.
Page 186: *Execution of Lount and Matthews* [Toronto Jail], Library and Archives Canada, C-001242.
Page 187: Robert O'Hara, *West Lodge n. of Queen St. W.,* Toronto Public Library, T 11429.
Page 188: C.W. Jefferys, from *The Picture Gallery of Canadian History Vol. 2,* p. 89, courtesy of the Jefferys Archive.
Page 189: *Toronto's First Industry* (c. 1815). 1934. Toronto Public Library, T 10884.

Page 190: From *Historical Etchings/Home Life*, the Crabtree Publishing Company, p. 28.
Page 191: From *Early Settler Children*, the Crabtree Publishing Company, p. 34.

Pages 192-193: Maps by Paul Heersink/Paperglyphs. Map data p. 192 © 2002 Government of Canada with permission from Natural Resources Canada.

Thanks to Barbara Hehner for her careful checking of the manuscript, and to Dr. Elwood Jones of Trent University, for his historical expertise on Upper Canadian religion and politics, and for his insights into the lively debate about the 1837 Rebellion.

This book is dedicated with love to my grandson David Lunn, newly launched on his teaching career.

The author would particularly like to thank Christopher Moore, Carol Martin, Jeffrey Kelly and my wonderfully unflagging editor, Sandy Bogart Johnston.

About the Author

When she was a child, Janet Lunn lived just outside a pre-revolutionary-war village in Vermont. "I used to daydream myself back to the time of that war," she says. "I wove long, elaborate stories for myself about ordinary people who were caught up in the struggle. In order to make my stories come alive, I read everything I could find (and could manage at that age) about that war." Janet came to Canada as a university student, married a Canadian and settled among the descendants of the refugees from that war. One of them was her husband.

"That old history looked different from this new perspective," she says. "I began making stories about these refugee families, stories that became published books. I read early Ontario history, I travelled to historic sites, I listened to songs, I visited archives. My husband and I wrote a history of United Empire Loyalist Prince Edward County. Nineteenth-century Ontario had come to feel like home." When she read William Kilbourn's book *The Firebrand*, about William Lyon Mackenzie and the 1837 rebellion in Upper Canada, Janet knew she wanted to write about a family involved in that rebellion. "I have, finally, done it with Arabella Stevenson's diary."

Janet loves the research that's needed for an historical story, seeing it as part detective work, part jigsaw puzzle. "The first part of the research for Arabella's story was easy. I found almost all I needed about the political struggle and the actual battles of the rebellion in books in my own library. What I had to really hunt for was city life in the Toronto of 1837–1838. What did the city look like then? How did the rich live? How did the poor manage? Most particularly, what were servants' lives like in the home of a wealthy family? What did they earn? What were their quarters like? What did they eat? Would the cook have a stove or would she still cook at a fireplace?

"My journey took me from the Internet, where I found virtual tours of splendid British houses, including the duties of every servant, to a real walk around old Toronto streets on the coldest day of winter — a walk that included a visit to The Grange at the Art Gallery of Ontario." Janet mined the Toronto Public Library's Baldwin Room for old books and diaries, the National Library and Archives in Ottawa for newspapers of the time, her local library in Ottawa, and used-book stores for obscure letters, diaries and books. "There was little to be found about servants' lives in Upper Canada except small, often vague references. Most Canadian writers of history, it seems, are more interested in backwoods pioneers and their hardships than in life in towns and cities.

"But there were nuggets of gold in unexpected places — in an obscure study of urban domestic servants in nineteenth-century Canada, on unexpected Web sites, in the old newspapers (where books, teachers, servants for hire and shipments of everything from fish to new hats were advertised). Eventually I either found what I needed or had to change my story to fit what I found. (I never did find exactly what Arabella would wear as a scullery girl so I had to guess — and I still feel the loss of a beautiful kitchen stove I found in a book about Victorian life, but for which I could find no reference before 1850.) Perhaps the most fun was checking in etymological dictionaries to make sure the words Arabella wrote in her diary were actually in use in 1838."

Janet thought that researching the political and military history would be the easy part, but it turned out to be the most difficult. "It appears that no two historians agree about all the reasons for the 1837 rebellions in the Canadas," she says. "Nor are dates consistent. For example, most sources give May 25 as the first date for prisoners in Toronto being sent to Fort Henry in Kingston. However, Samuel Thompson, in his *Reminiscenses of a Canadian Pioneer,* gives the date June 8, as remembered by one of the prisoners. I've gone with the prisoner. For one prisoner, I've found four different dates, in four separate accounts, for departure to Kingston. I've settled on the most likely.

"The research was, as it always is, a wonderful adventure. It gave me a trip back to a critical moment in our history from which I have returned, feeling as though I really have spent time with the people, great and small, on whose lives the city, the province and our country have been built."

Janet is the author of over a dozen books, from novels to picture books to *the* reference book for middle-grade students of Canadian history, *The Story of Canada,* which she co-authored with Christopher Moore. She won the CLA Book of the Year for Children Award for *The Root Cellar,* the Canada Council Prize for *Shadow in Hawthorn Bay,* and the 1998 Governor General's Award for Children's Literature for *The Hollow Tree.*

Janet is a member of the Order of Ontario and the Order of Canada. She is also the recipient of the Vicky Metcalf Award for Body of Work. In 2006 she received the Matt Cohen Award: In Celebration of a Writing Life. The committee citation for the award called her "a beautiful writer and a meticulous researcher" and commended her "leading role in the flowering of literature and the arts in Canada, especially of Canadian children's writing."

Copyright © 2006 by Janet Lunn.

All right reserved. Published by Scholastic Canada Ltd.
SCHOLASTIC and DEAR CANADA and logos are trademarks
and/or registered trademarks of Scholastic Inc.

National Library of Canada Cataloguing in Publication

Lunn, Janet, 1928-
A rebel's daughter : the 1837 rebellion diary of Arabella
Stevenson / Janet Lunn.

(Dear Canada)
ISBN 0-439-96967-0

1. Canada--History--Rebellion, 1837-1838--Juvenile fiction.
I. Title. II. Series.
PS8573.U55R42 2006   jC813'.54   C2006-901086-2

No part of this publication may be reproduced or stored in a retrieval system,
or transmitted in any form or by any means, electronic, mechanical,
recording, or otherwise, without written permission
of the publisher, Scholastic Canada Ltd.,
604 King Street West, Toronto, Ontario M5V 1E1, Canada. In the case of
photocopying or other reprographic copying, a licence must be obtained from
Access Copyright (Canadian Copyright Licensing Agency), 1 Yonge Street,
Suite 1900, Toronto, Ontario M5E 1E5 (1-800-893-5777).

6 5 4 3 2 1   Printed in Canada   06 07 08 09 10

The display type was set in Sexsmith.
The text was set in Garamond.

First printing June 2006